MW00944870

The Gnome King

The Elemental Kingdom
Book 1: EARTH

by Pamela Sue Hickein

Illustrations by Siang Yang Ng

Copyright ©2017 by Pamela Sue Hickein
Cover design and illustrations by Siang Yang Ng

ISBN-13: 978-1981956647
ISBN-10: 1981956646

All rights reserved. No part of this document may be
reproduced or transmitted in any form or by any means,
electronic, mechanical, photocopying, recording, or otherwise,
without prior written permission.

Printed in the United States of America.

FROG & TURTLE
CHILDREN'S PRESS

Dedication

For Benjamin, George and Mary—
creative children who inspired this
adventure while homeschooling
together in Malaysia.
For William and Frederick
who started our fairytale.

Thank you!

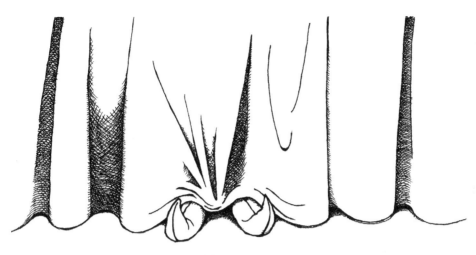

Chapter 1

A Little Surprise

Mary was reading her fairy book in the sun room where the tall Victorian windows allowed light to flood in. As she turned the first page, she heard a scuffle of little feet beneath her.

She looked down. She looked behind her.

"Reading about fairies must have made me think that fairies were real!" she said under her breath. She went back to her book.

"Ouch" she heard a tiny voice cry. She put down her book and looked again. A careful view revealed two tiny feet sticking out from under the window curtain.

She slowly rose up and tiptoed out of the room to where her brother George and cousin Ben were studying. They all home schooled together and the boys were working hard on their

Math equations.

"Shhh..." whispered Mary. "Don't say a word. Just come with me. I think we have a fairy in the house."

George and Ben stared at each other in joking disbelief. "A fairy, indeed!" their expressions seemed to say. But Ben and George were scientists first, so they quietly rose and crept back to the sun room to investigate.

Mary silently pointed to the curtains. Sure enough, two feet protruded out from beneath the fabric. They were tiny feet, covered in tiny green shoes.

Ben pulled out his magnifying glass and crept closer. The shoes were leather-looking slippers that were joined at the seams with tiny bits of thread.

"Remarkable!" he sighed under his breath. The shoes instantly disappeared, having been pulled back behind the curtains by their small owner.

Mary realized that they startled the fairy. "Oh, it's okay, little fairy," she hummed in a motherly way.

They all waited a moment.

No response.

George said, "Maybe he's afraid of us."

"I am most definitely NOT afraid of you!" cried a small man, who lifted the curtain and walked right out before them. He was clothed all in green with a little pointed hat.

He had a grey beard and mustache. He looked like a teeny, tiny grandfather fairy.

"Why, what a preposterous notion—to be afraid of three human babies!"

"Hey, we're not babies!" defended Ben. The little fairy scowled.

"Well, I'm not going to stand around here and argue with you babies. I have grown up fairy work to do," and he stomped off toward the kitchen and slipped outside through a tear in the screen.

Chapter 2

The Children's Secret

George, Ben and Mary looked at each other in amazement. They couldn't believe what they had just seen.

They had read about fairies—indeed, Mary was reading about fairies just that very day. But never in their lives had they dreamt that they would encounter any such creatures. The boys' scientific minds had not allowed them to believe that mystical creatures were real.

Mary peered out through the kitchen window.

"I wonder where he lives…" she pondered aloud. The boys joined her as she looked out.

Their backyard was large and full of little play areas they loved to explore. There were two vegetable gardens, with flower patches surrounding the house and garden shed. Their mother loved roses and herbs, so the yard was full of color.

Little pathways led from one garden to the next, with a patch of fir trees lining the far back edge. It was a miniature forest, with pine needles and cones covering the soft ground underneath it.

Father had tied a swing to one of the trees at the front edge of the forest patch. The children loved to go there to swing.

"Children!" Grandma McGillicutty called. She was an adopted grandmother who cared for them.

"Time for dinner!" she continued as she walked in from the dining room. "Your places are set, except for the silverware and drinks."

She turned to Mary, "Can you set the silverware on the table, dear?"

She put her hands on the boys' shoulders. "Ben, can you get glasses? George, can you bring cool water to the table and fill the glasses? You children are such a blessing to be so good at helping me."

The children jumped into action, although their minds were still on the little fairy.

"Do you think that there are more fairies outside?" Mary asked the other boys once Grandma McGillicutty went into another room. "Should we tell Grandma?"

"How do you know he was a fairy?" answered Ben. "I didn't see any wings."

"What else could he be?" Mary questioned.

"He could be an elf," George offered. "And I'm not sure we should tell the grown-ups. From what I've read, fairies trust children and allow themselves to be seen by us—but not adults." He shook his head.

"No, if you want to see the fairies again—or whatever they are," he said with a nod to Ben, "then we'd better keep it our little secret."

"Agreed?" Ben said, looking at Mary firmly.

"Agreed!" said Mary "but why are you looking at me? You know I would never say a word!"

"Okay," he kindly replied.

Ben and George looked at each other and winked. They knew Mary had a hard time with secrets, but somehow they knew that she would help keep this one—if she wanted to see a fairy creature again.

Chapter 3

The Library

After dinner, Ben and George ran to the library where the encyclopedia set filled the top shelves. From the top of the ladder, they looked for the volumes containing "E" for elf, "F" for fairy, "M" for mystical creatures, and "G" for gnome. They were hoping to find pictures that could help identify their newfound "friend."

George was just a little bit the taller of the two, so he was elected to reach up and hand each volume down to Ben. Each volume was heavy and dusty. They had probably not been used since their fathers were boys.

Nowadays, the boys used their computers to look up anything they might wish to know. But as they were not allowed on the computer until their home schooling was done, they decided to find out more the old-fashioned way: books!

Ben sat down with the "E" volume. He blew off the dust and sneezed immediately afterwards. "Atchoo!" He blinked his eyes until the dust cleared.

"God bless you!" Grandma McGillicutty said as she entered the room. "My goodness! What are you boys up to?" she wondered as she took a damp cloth from her apron and wiped down the books for them. "Why, I haven't seen these books out in ages, it seems! What are you looking up?" she asked.

"Oh, we're doing research, said George.

"Huh?" Ben looked at him, then received a stern gaze back. "Oh!" he seemed to remember. "Yes," he nodded. "Research!"

"What about?" she queried.

"Fairies!" Mary shouted as she joined them.

"Mary!" Ben and George said in unison. She put her hand over her mouth, then she resumed. "…for research!" she clarified.

Grandma McGillicutty's eyes twinkled. "I see…" she smiled. "Well, in that case, I've got a better book for you to use for your research." The children looked at each other. Grandma's eyes scanned the library shelves until they rested on a large book near the end of the top row.

"George, slide your ladder down to the end. You'll want that thick brown book there." She pointed as George and Ben picked up the ladder. The large, heavy book was soon in her hands. She wiped it off with her cloth.

"That's better," she sighed.

The children looked at the cover. It was gleaming with gold lettering. The Elemental Kingdom was written in large, ornate letters reminiscent of something they'd seen in books from J.R.R. Tolkien.

"We've never seen that book before," mused Ben. He and George were avid readers and they had read almost every book in the library two or three times!

"Well," began Grandma McGillicutty, "there's something interesting about this book. It seems that it is hard to find and doesn't turn up until you're ready to read what is inside..." She smiled to herself.

"Now, children, I must go back to the kitchen. I have cookies that are baking and I want to make sure that they come out at just the right time. Let me know when you'd like to take a break from your studies for a glass of milk and chocolate chip cookies, okay?"

"Okay!" the children resounded unanimously.

Chapter 4

The Elemental Kingdom

The children huddled around the library table. They opened up the book to the very first page. The paper was yellow and weathered by time. The words were all handwritten in ink, with colorful designs.

"Gosh, this book must be really old," Ben whispered.

"Let's see if it has a table of contents," George said as he turned the page.

They read together:

> Long ago, mankind lost contact with the elemental kingdom.
>
> This kingdom governs every natural process in the earth world.

This book was written to help mankind reclaim their knowledge of the unseen beings who help them.

Although they can no longer safely coexist, the hope is that someday, through the efforts of man to become a kinder, more peaceful race, they will see the elemental kingdom once more and live in harmony.

To all who may choose to be aware of the hidden kingdoms of the earth, be advised that there are four elemental substances with guardians that govern them according to the natural cycles and rhythms of sun and moon time.

The four elemental kingdoms are: fire, air, water and earth.

The elemental guardians are:

Salamanders – the guardians of fire

Sylphs – the guardians of the air

Undines – the guardians of water

Gnomes – the guardians of earth

Beside each guardian was an illustration.

"There!" Mary cried excitedly. "That's who we saw!"

"A gnome." Ben confirmed. "I knew it wasn't a fairy. Fairies aren't even listed here."

"But that looks like one," Mary put her finger on the sylph. Ben studied it.

"You're right, Mary." He considered for a moment. "It could be that they use the word 'sylph' instead."

"I'm re-reading the beginning," George slowly read the words: "Long ago, mankind lost contact with the elemental kingdom."

"Well," he paused. "I wouldn't believe it unless I saw a gnome for myself today."

"I know what you mean," Ben nodded. "This merits investigation."

"...and cookies!" Mary squealed with delight as the scent of freshly baked chocolate chip cookies filled the room. "Let's go!"

Soon, the room was empty. Only one old, large book remained open on the library table.

Then it vanished.

Chapter 5

Out in the Sunshine

"Why don't you take your cookies and milk outside into the sunshine and play while I clean up the kitchen, children." Grandma McGillicutty didn't need to say that twice. The children scooped up the warm cookies and dashed out into the garden.

"Where do you think he lives?" Mary asked as she found a pretty spot by the rose bed. From where she was sitting, she could see the vegetable garden paths and the strawberry planters.

Ben sat down next to her. "I don't know how we could know without exploring—but we'll need to know a few things before we start looking," he said as he took a bite of his cookie. It melted in his mouth.

He continued, "For example, what does he eat? And what type of home does he live in?" He took another bite—this time a big one and he silently thought while chewing.

"Right," George followed. "He'd need to live near a food source. He would need a house that would keep him safe from any predators, like owls or cats—he's a little guy. Anything could eat him."

"Eat him!" Mary's face went white.

"No," George corrected himself. He had forgotten that a lady was present. He thought, and smiled to himself. "He wouldn't let that happen. He's too clever for that, Mary—I'm just saying: what type of house would he build for himself that would prevent that sort of thing."

Mary sighed in relief. "Well, maybe there are others. In my fairy book, the fairies live in villages amongst the flowers and sometimes they live in hollowed-out mushrooms!"

"And there are different kinds—rose fairies, lavender fairies, daisy fairies—all sorts."

"Mary," Ben stopped chewing. "We're not talking about fairies. Those stories are written about things people think they know. We're trying to find a gnome—something that none of us has read about."

He looked at his cookie longingly, but decided to finish his point instead. "And I don't think that there are lavender gnomes…"

Mary giggled.

"…or rose gnomes," George smiled.

"Okay," Mary agreed. She looked up at George.

"George! Your face is covered with chocolate. And look at all those cookie crumbs on your lap!" She looked around and picked a large leaf from a nearby rhubarb plant.

"Here," she offered the leaf as a napkin. George wiped his face. Then he looked down and put the rest of the crumbs on the leaf and set it down while he got up to stretch.

Chapter 6

The Search

"Let's split up," George suggested.

"OK, but let's make sure we're thorough." Ben remarked as he took out a small notebook and tore two pages from it. "Here is a page for Mary—write down anything you see that might be important." He handed her a page with a pencil from his shirt pocket. "Here's one for you, too, George."

George took his piece of paper and took a pencil out of his back pocket.

"OK, thanks," he said. "Well, I think we need to look for three things at each area, looking at it from a small person's point of view. We need to assess food, water and any type of shelter which might be available to a little person like that."

"Um, sorry, George—what is shelter?" Mary asked.

"It's any place where the gnome might be able to make a home for himself," Ben explained.

"Yes," George agreed. "Somewhere to stay dry when it rains and to be safe from animals or… even people!"

"It would have to be away from lawn mowers, too" Ben added thoughtfully—thinking of his Saturday chores.

"Okay…" Mary sounded unsure. "But I'm not really clear about what I'm looking for…" her voice trailed off.

"Should I look for flower patches and mushrooms?" she looked eagerly at them.

"Mary!" the boys chorused, looking at each other with the secret facial signal, which seemed to say "Humph! Girls!"
But Mary didn't hear them, she had already begun her search for flowers and mushrooms and places far beyond where the lawn mower trims the grass. They could hear her singing sweetly as she looked from flower to flower.

The boys winked at each other, then got serious.

"Okay, do we know what we're looking for, then, Ben?" George had his list ready.

"Yes," Ben replied. "But I think that our search should be a little, well, quieter than Mary's. She's so loud, she's going to let him know she's coming!"

"Right," George smiled. "If we're quiet, we just might have a chance of seeing him again."

They each set out in different directions, carefully scanning low ground.

George went to the first vegetable garden and lay down in the middle of the squash patch. He watched ladybugs and butterflies and peered through the vines and leaves. Were there holes in the ground where he could hide? Were there any plants that could be hollowed out for a home?

Ben went to the small forest of fir trees at the back edge. He walked slowly and looked down to observe every little thing on the ground. He saw cones and fir needles and light brown earth and mushrooms.

He smiled to himself, thinking how pleased Mary would be at the sight of that.

Chapter 7

A Discovery

Ben lay down on the soft brown earth. He could smell the earthy fresh soil that he loved to breathe in during nature walks with his Dad. He thought about how his Dad would be helpful to him now, if he were near. He loved nature and could spot details that not many people could see.

He closed his eyes and listened to the wind in the trees above him. He heard the birds chirp to one another. Then he heard something else.

It sounded to him as if he heard clinking.

"Clinking?" he thought to himself. Yes, it was clinking.

He opened his eyes. Everything looked the same.

He looked around him. Nothing was different. Everything was the same—there were the patches of soft brown earth, fir needles, cones, mushrooms… but now he could no longer hear the sound.

He closed his eyes again. Nothing.

"Hmmm," he thought. "I'd better write this down: Forest area – clinking sound, then it stopped."

He looked around again.

"Food source nearby, if you go to the garden. Water is near the garden, too. Shelter…" he stopped.

He looked around again.

At the base of each tree was thick bark that covered the trunk. Some of the bark had craggy openings.

Something stirred above him. He looked up in time to see a squirrel disappear into a crevice in the bark of the tree.

"Shelter is possible within the trees," he wrote. He got up to go back to see what the others had found.

Initially, George had made his observations while lying on his stomach in the middle of both vegetable gardens. He smelled like chocolate and soon ants were all over him from every direction.

He decided to get up and view the garden from the air.

As he carefully examined the sweet peas, in the corner of his eye he would see the carrot tops waver, as if they were swaying in a quick breeze. Then, when he looked at the carrot tops, the chard leaves would move. As he switched his visual focus from vegetable to vegetable, he could see movement from the corner of his eyes.

"Curious!" he thought. "I'd better write that down."

"Children!" Grandma McGillicutty called from the kitchen door. "It's time to come in and wash up for dinner!"

George, Mary and Ben all came running from different corners of the yard. Just as they ran up the stairs, Mary looked back.

"George!" she called. "Did you clear away the cookie crumbs from the rhubarb leaf?"

"No," he called back.

"They are all gone!" she exclaimed as she held up the large, now-polished, clean leaf.

"I think someone ate your cookie crumbs!" she surmised.

Ben and George looked at each other knowingly.

"I think we found a food source," Ben smiled.

They went inside.

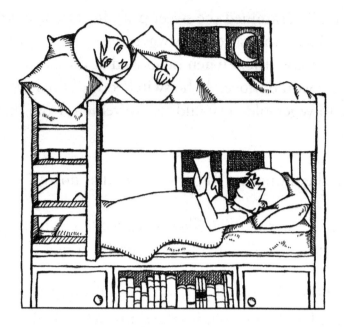

Chapter 8

Comparing Notes

Later that night, the children finished the rest of their schoolwork, helped Grandma McGillicutty wash and put away the dishes, and ran upstairs. This was their usual reading time. Ben and George shared a room upstairs.

George's Dad had made a bunk bed for them. Ben had the bottom bunk and George had the top. They could each see the backyard from their places on the bed.

"Okay, George." Ben began.

"You looked at the vegetable gardens, right? What did you write down about your area?"

"Well," George said as he took his paper out of his back pocket.

"George," Ben interrupted jokingly. "You have chocolate on your paper! How are you going to read that?!"

"I can see it fine," George insisted dryly. "I could see that food and water were ample if you lived with the vegetables, but that could be a problem because they get watered so often, and picked and weeded. You'd have to worry about people seeing you all the time. I could not see any place where it would be safe to live. I did see an underground burrow, but I'm not sure it would be safe or dry—especially when the sprinklers are on."

"But it's funny," he hesitatingly added, "As I looked carefully at one section of the garden I could have sworn I saw something move from the corner of my eyes. But when I looked toward that direction, I didn't see anything at all."

"We have to note everything," Ben insisted. "George, we saw an actual gnome today. If we're going to find him—or others like him—we need to be really observant."

"You're right," George agreed. "And I keep thinking about what the book said: that they have been around for years but we're not able to see them because mankind has done something wrong. All the wars we've been in and everything. Why can't we just get along?"

"I know…" Ben was quiet. That day's history lesson was about Sparta. They had read that the Spartans only let their children live if they could fight to stay alive. All people in Sparta served in the army.

He shook his head to clear his thoughts. "My area was interesting. The forest itself was quiet and shaded. There wasn't much to note except that when I lay down for a moment, I thought I heard…" he stopped.

"Heard what?" George asked.

"You're going to think I'm crazy, but I thought I heard clinking."

George hung his head down over the top bunk. "Clinking?"

"I know. It sounds strange, but I heard clinking, like if you were hitting two spoons together—but a higher pitch."

"You mean," added George, "a higher pitch—like tiny spoons hitting together?"

Ben stopped to consider this. He replayed the sound in his head.

"Yes," he replied.

Chapter 9

Mushrooms and Flowers

"Well! No one asked me what I wrote down!" Mary said from the doorway. She had been standing at the entrance, listening to the conversation.

"Okay, Mary," George smiled. "Show us what you've got."

Mary walked over to the bunk bed. She sat down on the carpet beneath them and held up her paper. On it were pictures of all the flowers in the flower and herb beds in each garden. She had a circle around some of the flowers, and an X over others.

"That's a picture of flowers!" George exclaimed.

"No, wait," said Ben, "Look closer."

George looked as Mary held her paper up.

"George, you asked me to find places where the gnome would be happy! So, I drew a picture of each flower. Then, I circled the ones that would be large enough for him to sit in—where the petals could hide him or cover him if it rained."

"Wow, Mary," Ben and George looked at each other. "That's pretty neat," they agreed.

"But I didn't know how to draw the fairy dust," she added. They blinked.

"Fairy dust?" Ben asked.

"Yes!" Mary shared. "It was sparkling around the mushrooms. It was like they were shining and glowing, like when I draw princesses with my glitter crayons."

"I didn't write down where the mushrooms were, but I remember them all." She looked up at the boys' faces.

They were enthralled by what she had to say.

"Shall I draw you a map?" she offered.

"Yes!" they said in unison.

They all followed Mary to her room where her art table waited complete with paper, markers, colored pencils, and glitter crayons.

Mary soon made a map of the entire backyard. George and Ben helped fill in areas she wasn't sure of. Then, the glitter crayons came out. Mushrooms were noted in every major area of the yard—from the vegetable gardens to the flower beds to the herb garden to the back porch steps, right outside the kitchen door.

"That..." pointed Mary to a glittery mushroom by the house, "is where George's cookie crumbs disappeared." They looked at each other in amazement.

Then, Ben remembered something.

"You forgot a few mushrooms, Mary," he said as he drew out his notebook. He penciled in a few mushrooms in the forest area.

They all smiled at each other.

Chapter 10

An Early Morning

Morning couldn't come fast enough for the children. They had decided to wake up early, get their schoolwork done and go out to the yard to investigate more. The children's parents would not be joining them for breakfast—they had to leave for a few days for a work project. Grandma McGillicutty would be in charge.

Ben's parents checked in with him by computer videoconferencing. He could see the Himalayan Mountains in the background while his Dad described the climate in Northern India.

They were happily exploring and he loved to listen to his Mom relate the stories of their travels. It was soon time for them to go to sleep and for him to start his day.

The children were finishing their math workbooks in the sun room when Mary looked down and saw two tiny feet at the base of the curtains once more.

She froze.

She wanted to tell Ben and George, but didn't know how without scaring the gnome away.

Then, an idea came to her.

"George, which page are you on now?" she asked softly. She hoped that he would look up and see her pointing at the gnome.

"Page 324," George said without looking up.

Mary's expression darkened. Then she had another idea.

"Ben, does this equation look right?" she asked even more softly.

Ben looked up to check the equation. He had often helped Mary with her math, but this time she was pointing down. He followed the invisible line from her finger to the bottom of the window.

He almost skipped a breath. He reached over and squeezed George's arm softly.

"Hey!" George bellowed.

The shoes disappeared.

Mary and Ben sighed in frustration.

Mary gently looked behind the curtain. There was no one to be seen.

"George!" Mary stood up and put her hands on her hips.

"What?" George looked at them, clueless. They were both glaring at him. He had no idea what he could have done.

"We just missed him, again!" Ben groaned. "We were so close!"

He was about to further lament, but then saw the yarn basket move from side to side momentarily. He put his finger to his lips to silence everyone, and then pointed to the basket.

George saw the tip of the gnome's hat sticking out from the balls of woolen yarn.

"Well, I'm not surprised," he continued to bellow in a bragging tone. "A little teeny weensy gnome is no match for us—he's afraid of human babies!"

"What?!" came a sharp reply from the yarn basket.

The gnome promptly crawled out. "Now, let us make this perfectly clear. I am not afraid of anyone or anything— especially not you human babies!"

He pointed at each one of them and looked them in the eyes to make sure they understood his meaning.

Chapter 11

The Gnome Code

"I am here for a noble reason," the elderly gnome directed his gaze solemnly to each one of the children. They sat down quietly, almost without a thought. The senior gnome commanded respect.

"The earth is changing and we need the help of human men to stop it," he said in a lowered voice. They all leaned nearer to hear better.

"Did you want to talk to my Daddy?" Mary asked him, wide-eyed with concern.

"Yes," he replied, "and his brother."

George and Ben looked at each other—the gnome knew their fathers and wanted to speak to them. It was too incredible.

"But why them?" George asked.

"What could they do?" Ben looked at the gnome. His father was on the other side of the world, for Heaven's sake, he thought.

"Your fathers knew us when they were young, like you," the gnome explained. "They pledged to protect us and help us at one time when we needed help. We helped them, too, although they may not have known it at the time. We taught them the ways of nature and they grew up to be good, honest men."

"But the problem we have now is much larger. All the elemental kingdoms are contacting human men of honor—whom they may have contacted when they were young—to refresh their memories of the elemental world and to enlist their help."

"What's wrong?" Mary cried. "Why do you need help?"

The gnome lowered his head.

"I cannot answer that, young miss. You will not understand the problem unless you know about the elemental kingdoms and all that they are and what we do. It is a long story—and one which gnomes are not allowed to disclose unless given permission from the High King."

"But, now I'm scared," Mary started to cry. "Daddy and Uncle Jeffrey are not here. Now, no one can help." George and Ben felt sad and alarmed, too, but instead of showing their feelings, they began to comfort Mary.

"Now, now, now," began the old gnome. "Do not cry. It makes

no sense to cry. It does not help."

"Maybe so," said George defiantly, "but she's just a little girl." Ben nodded in agreement.

Ben thought about something his Mom said on the videophone that day—that even though he was young, he was wise and courageous and to believe in himself. "Can we help?" he asked the gnome.

The gnome looked at the children.

He thought for a moment.

"Very well," said the gnome. "I will take you to the High King, but, little miss…" he said while looking directly at Mary.

"Yes?" she stopped sniffling and looked back.

"If you want to help, you will need to be brave. Can you do that?" he asked her.

Mary pondered a moment. "Could I be brave?" she asked herself.

"Yes," she affirmed.

Chapter 12

The Green Mouse

"Then, you will all see the King." The grandfatherly gnome decreed.

"He lives far away. We'll need to trek by moonlight so we will not be seen." The gnome considered for a moment. "Go about your day as if nothing has occurred. I will be back after the sun has set. Be ready to go."

"Should we bring anything with us?" Ben asked.

"Yes," he replied. "Bring water and food. The journey will be long." The gnome nervously looked around. "I must go now," he said and then slipped out through the hole in the kitchen's back-door screen.

"Oh my goodness!" the children heard Grandma McGillicutty

cry out from the kitchen. They looked at each other.

"Did she see him?" they wondered as they looked at each other.

They ran to her.

When they got to the kitchen, she was holding her chest, breathing heavily. "Are you okay, grandma?" Mary asked as she ran to hug her. "Are you all right?" Ben repeated. He took a mop from her hand so that she could sit down.

"Oh my goodness," she repeated. "George," she said looking straight at him, "We need to find those mouse traps..." and then she stopped to catch her breath. The boys sighed in relief. They smiled at each other. She thought the gnome was a mouse!

"Sure," George said as walked toward the door. "I'll get them now. I think they're in the shed." He paused and looked at Ben, "Ben, do you want to help me?" Ben knew that was secret code for 'Ben, come with me so we can talk privately.' He jumped up and the two went out the door.

"Are you okay?" Mary asked Grandma McGillicutty again. "Oh, yes, dear. Just surprised. Believe me, in my time, I've seen thousands of mice, honey." She gave Mary a loving squeeze to reassure her.

"Except..." she continued, "now you're going to think this strange, and maybe I'm just getting old, but I could have sworn... I could have sworn..."

She looked toward the door, and tried to continue her sentence, "that this particular mouse had a pointed hat and little green clothes."

She looked at Mary. Mary gulped and then hugged Grandma McGillicutty again so she couldn't see her face. She didn't know what to say! She had to keep their secret.

Back in the garden shed, George and Ben were shuffling through pots and planters looking for the box mousetraps. They finally found two behind a few bags of fertilizer.

The boxes were made of metal and had a little entry hole for mice to crawl into, a place for cheese, and a little door that closed behind them. George's Dad had used them before to catch mice and drive them out to the nearby forest reserve to release them—far away from the tasty crumbs available in Grandma McGillicutty's kitchen.

Chapter 13

In the Garden Shed

Old rags hung on hooks over the planting table in the shed. As the boys used them to clean the traps, George finally spoke. "Ben, I'm not sure what we're going to come up against on our journey tonight. I didn't want to alarm Mary, but I think we will need to be prepared for anything."

"What do you mean?" asked Ben, polishing the outside of the metal box.

"Well…" George began to think out loud, "the gnome didn't want to be seen… didn't want to be seen by who?"

"Who or whom?" Ben questioned.

They had begun to learn the difference between who and whom in yesterday's language lesson.

"Ben! This is no time for a grammar lesson." George looked at him sternly.

"Okay," Ben conceded, "So, *who* do you think he might be talking about?"

"I don't know." George replied. "That's just it." He looked directly at Ben. "We don't know."

"Well, then," Ben paused as he looked around the shed, "we'll need to be able to defend ourselves."

"Exactly." George agreed.

They started to look around the shed for lightweight tools that they could use to defend themselves or make shelter should they need to be away for more than a day. They tested the strength and weight of their various hiking sticks, looked through the shovels and trowels and various sundry items that had been in the shed for ages.

Under the window stood a wooden box full of hedge trimmers, jars of nails and screws and bits of wood. Ben decided to sort through it and began to move things around to see what he could find. At the bottom of the old box he found a handle.

"That's strange," Ben remarked as he pulled on it. "It's attached to the bottom."

George had found an old Swiss army knife and had been sharpening the ends of some of the hiking sticks. He came over to look. Sure enough, the handle was attached to the bottom of the box just as if it were...a door!

Both boys looked at each other with the same conclusion.

They started pulling the items out until it was quite empty. On the inner edges of the box ran a line of space. The bottom was not attached to the side of the box. They tried to lift up the box, but it wouldn't move! They carefully examined the base and found that it was attached to the floor.

George reached in and pulled the handle, the bottom of the box began to shift and move. Ben reached in to help. Finally, it came loose and flew up into the air. The boys fell back with the bottom of the box right on top of them.

Chapter 14

Like Fathers, Like Sons

George coughed at the dust. Ben blinked. They looked at each other and then raced to the box. They looked inside.

"Oh," Ben gasped.

"Holy smoke," George exhaled.

Inside the box they could see deep, deep down into a hole. On closer view, they realized it could be a room. They could see a flattened dirt floor, little bits of carpet and some wooden pieces of furniture, but they could not see anything clearly for there were several inches of thick, dark grey spider webs obscuring their view.

"I'm not going in there!" Ben was looking straight at the cobwebs.

George grabbed the longest hiking stick and put it into the hole. He stirred around, as if he were mixing a stew. The webs caught hold of the stick and soon were spun on the end, like cotton candy.

Ben could now see ahead. "Hey!" he exclaimed. "That's my Dad's name!"

On a small table below was a leather bag with the word Jeffrey burned onto it. Next to it lay a spyglass, a compass, two sling shots, another bag and more… but they couldn't quite see what else.

"Well, Ben." George smiled as they looked at each other. He pointed down. "There are our tools!"

Ben smiled back. "Yes, but why is my Dad's name on the bag?"

"The gnome did say that my Dad and yours knew him. They never told us that, right?" George reasoned.

Ben nodded.

"Well, maybe that's not all they didn't tell us," he said while he reached for the ladder. It was hanging on the side of the wall. They lowered the ladder down into the hole. It was the perfect fit for the box and leaned up against the top of the box while firmly touching the ground below.

"Okay, here goes," George said as he lowered himself down.

Some of the steps of the ladder creaked. He shifted his weight to the next step. It began to crack. Ben snickered. "That's one too many chocolate chip cookies," he teased. George smiled. They teased each other like brothers all the time.

Finally, he was on the ground. He looked around. He drew a slow breath. "Ben, you've got to see this. There are hand-drawn maps on the walls, there's some candles, some flint," he kept scanning the room. "Wow, here's another bag. Look, Ben!"

He lifted it up for Ben to see. The word Brent was on its side, burned into the leather.

"Your Dad!" Ben exclaimed.

"Boys!" Grandma McGillicutty called from the kitchen door.

"Time for lunch!"

"Okay," Ben called back. "George, you'd better put all the tools you can see into the bags and come up quickly." Then he thought for a moment. "And bring the maps—just lay them on top of each other, roll them up and hand them to me."

He heard George scurry for a moment and then up popped the scroll of maps. Ben grabbed them, and then stepped back. Several careful creaks later, up came George, too. He had two fully packed bags and a big smile on his face.

Ben had a feeling that now they were ready for their adventure.

Chapter 15

Maps

George brought the animal traps into the kitchen while Ben snuck the supplies to their bedroom by the back stairs.

Mary was coloring at her table in her bedroom. She saw Ben cross the hallway. She followed him into the boys' room.

"May I come in?" she asked from the doorway. Ben and George had requested she not barge in. She hadn't always remembered to stop and ask, but she was feeling especially conscientious today.

"Okay, Mary," Ben replied while he emptied the bags onto the floor. There was a compass, flint, Swiss army knife, maps, a spyglass, candles… he decided that he'd better start organizing the pile to make a quick inventory. He got out his notebook and pencil.

"What's this?" Mary asked as she picked up the scroll of maps.

"They're maps that we found," Ben answered, still organizing. He wasn't sure if he should tell her about the underground room they had found. He had put everything back so that no one would find it.

Mary unrolled the maps and set each one out on available floor space. One map showed stars in the sky. One map showed a forest with lines leading from one area to another. The third map showed something quite familiar to her.

"I'll be right back!" She ran to her room and came back with her own map of the backyard.

"Look, Ben!" she said. She put her map up beside the last map on the floor. He came over. "Oh, wow, Mary," he said as his eyes went from one to the other.

They were both maps of the backyard. The one on the floor had more detail—there were tunnels running beneath the gardens and they seemed to be connected by the mushrooms. Some tunnels stopped at the mushrooms.

"Are the mushrooms doorways?" Ben pondered aloud.

"They might be elevators!" Mary giggled.

"Mary!" Ben looked at her seriously, but then his eyebrows lifted and he looked back at the map. "Hey, maybe they are." He took a closer look. He ran his finger from mushroom to mushroom.

"If they are passageways, then they couldn't be on the surface. There's too much digging and watering on the topsoil," he realized.

"I'm sorry for that look, Mary. You could be right."

Mary didn't know what to say. She was very glad to be right, even almost right. She smiled admiringly at Ben.

"Hey! You guys are missing some great chocolate cake," George struggled to say. His mouth was full. He was watching them from the doorway. Grandma McGillicutty had rewarded him for setting the animal traps with an early helping of dessert.

All of a sudden he saw what they were musing over—the maps. He stepped in to get a better look.

Chapter 16

By the Light of the Moon

Night had fallen quickly that evening. If they simply had nothing to do but wait for the sun to set, the day would have gone by slowly. But the children had many things to do.

They had finished their schoolwork—Math, Language, History, Science and Geography. Mary helped Grandma fold laundry. George cleaned the fireplace. Ben cut up firewood.

Grandma McGillicutty never once noticed that each one took turns running to the rooms upstairs to fill their backpacks. She didn't notice the missing blueberry muffins, or giant pretzels, apples or raisin buns. She didn't think it odd that Mary had gotten out the children's water bottles, then washed and dried them. Sometimes the children brought their water bottles into the garden.

But, she did look more carefully at the kitchen floorboards that day, in case the odd little mouse had returned.

At the end of the day, she had hugged and kissed the children and bid them good night.

She quietly poured herself a cup of tea and looked out onto the tranquil night sky. A single moon shone down to reveal the garden and all its detail.

"It's the end of a good day," she sighed.

Mary was looking at the garden, too. From the upstairs bedroom window she could see a vast fairyland, complete with hidden tunnels and elevators. "It's the beginning of an exciting night!" she thought.

Her backpack was full of goodies. She didn't know what the boys had packed, but she knew all that she had was absolutely necessary. She had included her pink hairbrush, hair ribbons, her doll and important bits of this and that.

"Ready?" she heard the boys whisper from the doorway.

"Yes," she answered back.

The boys each had their backpacks on. They were full, but light. The maps were tied to Ben's backpack, safely contained in a canvas telescope case.

Mary put her backpack over her shoulder. They tiptoed down the stairs. George looked around the doorway to the kitchen to see if Grandma was still at the table. All was still and quiet. The coast was clear.

They were about to go to the sun room to meet the gnome when something stirred near the back door. They heard Thomas, their cat, meow. "Back!" cried a stout little voice.

Ben opened the door. Mary scooped Thomas up in her arms. There stood the old gnome with his hands on his hips.

"We're ready!" George whispered. The gnome waved them forward toward the garden, motioning for them to follow him.

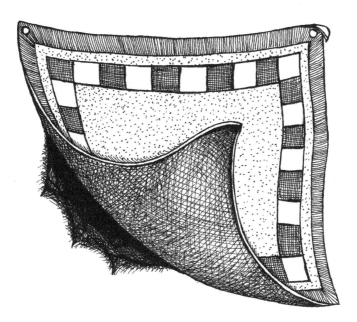

Chapter 17

The Great Forest

The moonlight illumined the tiny figure as he led the way. Though he was small, he was fast! He zipped to the garden shed in a flash. The children followed.

Inside, the box was glowing.

"Remove the contents and open up the bottom of the box," the gnome instructed. "Our ways to the Great Forest are too small for you. You'll have to take the passages built by man long ago—ones your fathers used to travel upon."

Mary put her hand over her mouth in astonishment as the boys moved quickly to empty the box and pull open the hidden hatch.

The gnome was slightly surprised to see that no further explanation was needed with the box.

Ben took down the ladder from the wall and started to lower it down.

"Don't worry, Mary," George said in a soothing voice, "it's okay to go down. I checked it out today. It's safe."

Ben was about to add that George had also cleared away all the cobwebs, but on second thought, he realized that perhaps he'd better not. Mary may not want to put one toe down there. He smiled to himself.

The lower room was now glowing with candlelight. They made their descent nimbly. George carried the gnome on his backpack. Crack. One of the steps finally fell apart. "I told you! Too many cookies," Ben teased from below.

Mary and Ben looked around. The room felt cool and damp. The walls were solid earth with patches of rock. The ceiling was made of thick, sturdy wooden beams. An old woven carpet hung down over the far wall, nailed in place to the ceiling above.

"There," the gnome pointed to the carpet. George walked closer, and pulled the rug aside. A dark entrance lay behind it— it seemed to be the beginning of a tunnel.

"There are torches that line the walkway, farther down a bit. We need to hurry and get into the tunnel so that we can blow these candles out. No one can know we're here," he explained.

Ben looked up. The ceiling hatch was still wide open.

The others had gone ahead into the tunnel. He took a candle, blew out the others and followed. He closed the carpet wall behind him.

They traveled for what seemed like hours. The gnome sat on George's shoulder, directing the way. Mary walked behind George, looking ahead to see what his candle revealed. Ben's light gave her courage from behind.

The tunnels were a series of underground walkways. Sometimes they could see the chip marks on the rocky walls where man had used force to hollow them out. They came across tunnels that met theirs and went off again.

"Who could have made these tunnels?" Ben spoke the question that the others were thinking.

Light began to shine from up ahead.

"Now," whispered the gnome, "put your candles out."

The children obeyed. The smell of candle smoke filled the air, clearing as they walked ahead.

Ben knew that Mary would be afraid. "It's okay, Mary" he said softly.

"I'm not afraid," protested Mary. They walked silently for a little while, then she slowed down. "Well, maybe I am, a little bit," she admitted.

George stopped at the end of the tunnel. Ben and Mary stood beside him. Before the children lay an enormous forest, full of leafy trees and the sounds of nocturnal animals.

"This is the Great Forest," the gnome announced. "We must venture to the heart of the woods to find the entrance to the High King's palace."

Chapter 18

Through the Trees

The gnome hopped off George's shoulder onto the ground. "From this point onwards, follow me. We will be running quickly from tree to tree."

He looked pensive. "It is imperative that you follow me to the exact tree," he emphasized the word 'exact.'

He saw the questioning looks from the children. "You see, some trees will shelter and protect us, but many will not. They are afraid to go against The Neutral Pact of the Great Forest Trees—that is to say that they know there are forces battling one another here. Nature has to change. And in this changing time, the trees have decided to resist. They are not allowed to help us."

"What war?" asked Ben.

The gnome looked serious for a moment. A hoot owl called in the distance.

"There's no time to explain," said the gnome, "Let me get you babies to safety. Follow me."

He dashed off to the first tree and hid beneath a low clump of branches. The children did the same. Then, he ran to the next. The children followed close behind.

They watched as the gnome carefully scanned the trees ahead, seemed to listen, and then moved forward quickly, passing several trees at once until he reached the right one. They continued in that way through the forest, waiting for a few minutes and then running at top speed to the safety of the next tree. Finally, they stopped.

The gnome began to silently communicate with trees for what seemed like a very long time.

He looked concerned. "There are no friendly trees for quite a distance," he whispered.

Then, he turned to the boys. "You will need to stay here for a little while until I can get help."

He asked the tree to lower his bottommost branches to form a tent-like covering for them.

"I will be back as soon as I can," he put his tiny hand on Mary's shoe. "You need to stay together and be very quiet. It might be a few hours, but I will return."

He then looked at all of them and ordered, "Do not leave the tree!"

He walked over to a mushroom at the base of the tree trunk, lifted it up as if it had hinges, and jumped inside. The mushroom automatically closed.

"I thought so!" exclaimed Ben excitedly. "Shhhhhhh..." The leaves of the tree seemed to say as the branches closed up more around them.

"I'm sleepy," Mary said quietly.

"I know what you mean, Mary," said Ben. His arms were still aching after the day's work of woodcutting. "I'm hungry," added George.

"George!" Ben and Mary whispered. George reached into his backpack and popped a granola bar into his mouth.

Chapter 19

Brave Escorts

The children huddled together in the leafy arms of the tree. Outside, they could hear the wind blowing, an occasional animal scurrying, and the hoot owls in the distance. Finally, the branches parted and a small grey mouse appeared in the clearing.

"I've come to find you and help you," he said, quite clearly, although he thought he might have to repeat himself, as the children were shocked into silence. He couldn't tell whether they understood him or not.

"I say," he repeated slowly, "I have come to help!"

"Ohhhh," Mary bent down to pet him. "You're just like the mouse in my picture book. You're so cute!" she said dotingly.

"We have no time for this!" said the mouse crossly.

"We have to leave immediately," he said. "They know you are here!"

"But, who knows we are here?" cried Ben and George together. The mouse ignored them. "Follow us—now!"

Outside the tree boughs was an army of mice—lined up in rows upon rows. In the middle was an open space. The mouse directed the children to that central space and then the animals began to run. The children kept up—with mice on either side, plus ahead and behind them.

Then, they heard a great fluttering sound. Above them in the night sky, a flock of pure white doves awakened from their slumber protected the children from the air.

They ran and ran and ran without stopping until Mary stumbled and fell. A great howl drew up from behind them.

"The wolves!" they heard the mice cry. George picked up Mary. Ben grabbed George's backpack and carried it for him. They began to run again.

Up ahead there was a great tree. This tree was larger than their house.

"How could such a tree exist?" the boys thought. Mary had her head on George's shoulder.

The howls grew louder from behind. The great tree opened its branches as if to receive them. George and Ben ran straight to it, aided by the mice.

The doves flew up and away, the mice disappeared through nearby burrows, and the children were swept close to the tree by giant tree boughs.

The branches of the tree were incredibly thick. Though the children felt the enormity of the protection the tree provided, they could still hear howling and scowling on the other side of the foliage. Wolves scratched and bit at the trees.

Mary began to silently cry, but George put his finger to her mouth so that she would try to stay silent.

"They know we're here," Ben explained. "They can smell us." The three huddled together, hugging each other.

"It's alright," spoke a familiar voice. The gnome had appeared beside them. "The Great Tree will protect us now," he said reassuringly. "Let us proceed."

Mary found that she could walk again. They followed him around the tree trunk until they reached a crevice in the bark. The gnome opened it as if it were a door. Light shone out as they entered. The door closed and the sounds of the wolves instantly ceased.

Chapter 20

The High King

Once inside the tree, they realized that they were in the middle of a great room. It was extremely bright. George looked around for a light source, but couldn't find one.

"Welcome to our home," a grandmotherly gnome seemed to appear from nowhere. "Please, please, sit down and rest a moment. You have traveled far and must be tired."

"And hungry!" Ben chimed in. He did not mean to sound ungracious, but when he was hungry, he was hungry!

The little woman smiled and laughed, "Yes, of course, and hungry." She pointed to a table laden with fruits and nuts, berries and juice, adorned with flowers. Mary ran to the table to smell the flowers.

The matronly gnome put a drop of flower essence into each cup from a golden goblet.

"This drop will help you recover from the fright that the wolves put into you! Those pestering creatures. Thank goodness the doves and mice were on call this evening for your safety."

The children sat and drank and ate heartily of all that was offered. As their tummies filled and their tension eased, they began to look around and notice things. The interior walls were magnificent. The wood seemed to be alive with light. The furnishings were of wood and all seemed connected to the tree itself. There were several doorways. In their hunger the children had not seen the gnomes leave the room.

The gnomes now rejoined them.

"I suppose we should know these babies by their names, Fiona."

George and Ben each made a face.

Mary kind of liked it. Being called a baby sounded cute and adorable.

"I'm Mary," she began. "…and this is my cousin Ben and my brother George."

"I am Queen Fiona," the grandmotherly gnome extended her tiny hand to each child with a smile.

"…and this is High King Hendrick." She said waving her hand to the little gnome.

"High King?" George questioned. "High King?!"

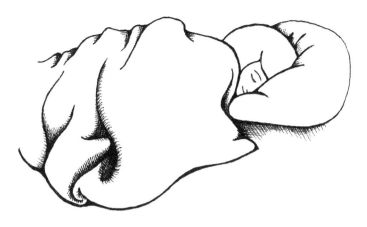

Chapter 21

Clearing Things Up

"You said that the High King was the only one that could explain what is happening," George looked at High King Hendrick. He wasn't sure if he should grimace with frustration or bow in reverence.

He decided he'd better clear things up. "Why wait until we are all the way out here to tell us?"

"Yes," Ben, added, "and why keep it a secret?"

"If you knew I was the king it would have put you in great danger," said High King Hendrick.

"Danger from what?" asked George and Ben together.

High King Hendrick answered, "Danger from the growing evil in the great forest. If you knew the truth of who I was, your thoughts would give us away."

"Gnomes are being taken as slaves and I'm afraid that there are only a very small number of us left. My people can no longer protect us. That is why you had to have a bodyguard of mice and doves. This evil extends beyond the great forest to all lands in the world," he said thoughtfully.

"It's time to explain," the King cleared his throat. He moved away from the table and motioned for the children to follow him.

The boys followed and then looked back.

"Where's Mary?"

George looked under the table. She had finished her meal, curled up on the floor, and had fallen fast asleep.

"Allow me to care for her," Queen Fiona cooed. "It's been a long time since we had a girl-child in the castle."

She carefully roused Mary and helped her over to a grand sofa where she then reclined and went back to sleep. The Queen covered her with a rose tufted blanket. A soft scent of wildflowers surrounded her.

Confident that Mary was well cared for, the boys followed the King. He led them through the northernmost doorway and up a tall series of stairs that wound in a spiral pattern to the top of the tree. At the top of the stairs, they entered another room.

Ben's eyes lit up. George exhaled a low whistle. As boys of technology, they were electrified with excitement.

The walls were circular and on each of the four directions were waist-to-ceiling computer screens—all showing data from what looked like across the globe. Each screen had a picture of the world; unlike any they'd ever seen. The topographical features— the high mountains, the low deserts, even changes in the ocean floor were accurately depicted by what might be holographic technology.

The three dimensional aspect amazed the boys. Ben removed his magnifying glass and walked toward the nearest screen to examine it up close. He put his hand through a mountain and touched the river nearby.

Strange.

He thought he felt water.

George walked toward the center of the room to look at a large intricately carved table that stood there. On the top of it was another computer map. He looked around the room from map to map…each one had different data.

The boys caught each other's gaze.

"Boy, would I love to have this for our home school!" George exclaimed.

"I could stay in here for days," smiled Ben. "This is MY kind of room!"

Chapter 22

The Water Kingdom

The High King began to give the boys a tour of the room, beginning with the North.

"This is the Great Room. There is one such room on every continent. For, although I am High King of the Gnome Kingdom, there are High Kings of each earthly kingdom with command centers throughout the world. We all consult each other to maintain the various systems of the earth."

"The natural world as we all know it, has four elemental kingdoms—fire, air, water, and earth (which includes metal)," he began. "There are beings who guard each kingdom."

He pointed toward the first screen, "This is the Water Kingdom."

On the northernmost wall, vast waterways appeared above, through and beneath the earth's crust. The boys studied it closely. It did not resemble any world maps they had ever seen.

Maps usually depict a surface view, but this was a multidimensional view of all water sources around the world. They could see oceans, waterways on land and deep underground. They saw that water covered every part of earth, even in the deserts where enormous rivers seemed to be buried several miles under the surface.

"The undines guard and monitor the waterways—well, as much as they are able," the High King continued. He touched a gemstone at the bottom of the screen. The screen changed to multiple screens containing live video of water nymphs—young maidens moving through different waterways and oceans.

As they moved, they waved their arms, purifying the water as they swam. Dolphins swam side by side with the ones in the ocean, as did whales. They were fast, but as they turned from side to side the boys thought that they saw fish tails.

Could it be possible? George and Ben looked at each other.

"Mermaids really exist?" they echoed.

The High King smiled. "That's very funny. Down here, we have to convince our children that human babies really exist!"

He touched another gemstone and the map reappeared.

"What are those green patches?" Ben asked. Amidst the waterways, various colors dotted the screen. Large green patches dominated some areas of the ocean.

"They are out-of-control algae growths," the King replied. "The yellow patches are where plastics and other types of garbage line the surface of the waters. They don't pollute the water underneath, but they do block out the sun, and that's a problem for life underneath."

"What about the orange?" George pointed to some of the coastlines and many of the rivers.

"These are waterways that have been polluted by toxic run-off or industrial waste," the King explained.

The boys had a sinking feeling. On closer look, they saw red areas in the middle of the oceans. Were they islands? They were too small to be ships.

The gnome, following their gaze, sadly continued.

"The red areas are called 'dead zones.' No life can exist in these areas because it is deplete of oxygen. If a fish swims in, it had better swim right out or else…" his voice trailed off.

Efforts are being made to clean everything up, and to advise the marine life about places where life is still sustainable, but the water quality of our earth is changing quickly.
"Is that why you need our fathers' help?" George asked.

"It's larger than even this," the High King frowned.

"Let's look at the next wall," he said as he walked toward the East. The boys were right behind him.

Chapter 23

The Air Kingdom

"This is the Kingdom of the Air and you might be surprised to know that this kingdom includes all plant life, most notably trees," the king announced, referring to the map on the eastern wall.

This screen was constantly moving. Clouds, even sand and dust flew across the screen according to present live-time atmospheric weather conditions.

Ben couldn't resist. He had to touch a puffy cloud. He poked a finger through a cumulus cloud system. It felt so real! And yet, he hadn't disrupted the visual picture.

He walked over to another area where rain clouds were

showering the land below. He touched them and pulled back his finger. On it were tangible drops of water. Ben showed George his finger. George gasped. He couldn't believe it! He scanned the map for a rainstorm near him. He touched it.

"Ouch!" he said and drew back instantly. He started to suck on his finger.

"Must have been lightning," the High King was amused at the boys' curiosity. "It won't hurt you, but I do not advise you to do that much more."

"If you are finished playing," he said with a twinkle in his eye, "we should check to see how the sylphs are doing."

He touched a gemstone at the base of the screen. It turned to several screens, featuring fairy-like creatures tending plants and overseeing weather systems to keep them alive.

"Look, George. There's Mary's fairies!" Ben smiled.

The High King looked at them. "There was a time when you believed in the unbelievable, too, I daresay. It's easier for us to communicate with small children than with older ones like you two."

"You need proof of who we are and what we do before you will help." He pointed to all the screens in the room.

"Little Mary would help us without any explanation. She's been playing with the sylphs for years. They are her little friends. Later, she will think that she has only dreamt them, but they are as real as you and I."

The boys looked surprised. They looked at each other and then back to the screen. It was hard to tell at first, but as they looked closely they saw small sylphs flying from tree to tree, flower to flower, bush to bush, checking leaf quality.

Large armies of sylphs were pushing cloud systems back and forth. On one screen, they could see butterflies helping the sylphs. They were flying side by side. This reminded them of the dolphins and undines.

The gnome pressed another gemstone and the scene turned to the world map again.

Chapter 24

The Wood Element

"Look, George," Ben pointed out. "This time the colors on the map make more sense."

They could see blue cool air at the North and South poles. The air looked redder as it warmed and flowed nearer to the equator. Color buoys showed digital data of the water—how the oceans warmed or cooled by the air temperature of prevailing winds.

There were also sensors across all the land. They leaned in to see and found that key trees were signalling back temperature data. There were red flags where temperatures were becoming too warm or too cold for certain species to survive.

"Remarkable," they thought.

"There's more," the King pressed a gemstone. Another layer of data covered the temperature codes with a new set of colors. The original temperature map faded, but was still visible so that all data could be viewed as a whole.

"This layer shows air composition—what the atmosphere is made up of in different areas of the world, " he began.

"But air is air," George looked at the king. "It's primarily made up of about 78% Nitrogen, and 20% Oxygen." "Right," Ben nodded, "with about 1 1/2% left over for carbon and other things…"

"Your fathers have taught you well," the King smiled. "Yes, air is air, but it's the percentages that are changing rapidly, and more carbon and other elements are disrupting the balance."

"Air composition determines air quality." He pointed to the map.

Large red patches loomed over the largest industrial cities on the map. The red air was quickly dispersed, following main wind currents of the earth. Red changed to orange, then to yellow and other colors as it swept throughout the world.
High mountain systems had white or light pastel-colored air indicators. Land systems nearer to sea level, especially those near large populations, contained air indicators that were darker in color.

Anticipating that they would ask what the colors meant, the

King explained, "The white areas are patches of air that are clean, well-balanced and nourishing for life.

"The yellow air has higher levels of certain elements due to being mixed with carbon-based exhaust from volcanoes, factories and vehicles."

"The orange air is more polluted. The red air can seriously harm life. The sylphs in these areas are working hard to stay in balance but not all the trees are cooperating. They have either resigned or joined forces with—" the King paused.

"Allow me to first finish showing you all the elemental kingdoms. As I said, only then can I explain what is happening. You will soon know about the forces we must challenge in order to bring balance to the world."

Chapter 25

The Fire Kingdom

As they wandered toward the southern wall, the boys quickly decided that they would NOT be touching this map!

The screen was hot.

The boys saw volcanoes—even where they had no idea volcanoes existed: deep under the world's oceans, even at the earth's icy poles, under thick glaciers.

They saw magma systems flowing throughout the world like bright red fiery rivers, deep underground.

"This is the Fire Kingdom," the King said as he touched a gemstone to bring up another layer. The atmospheric weather patterns instantly appeared. This time, it contained only the points where hot and cold air systems met. Lightning lit up the screen from several points on the map.

"The fire elementals supervise the heating of the earth, lightning from the skies above and magma movement from the depths of the mantle beneath the earth's crust," the King used his hands to bring the boys attention to the lightning.

"Many believe fire to be a destructive force, and it certainly can be, but when lightning strikes the earth, it changes nitrogen in the soil into a form that plants can use to live. It also charges the air with ions. Any fire that is created can sometimes bring life, too. Pinecone seeds will not emerge until the outer portion has burned."

"Volcanoes will unexpectedly erupt, but they have a reason for doing so. They move the earth and combine rocks, melting them down to form new substances we need for our jobs on the earth."

The King pressed another gemstone. A new layer swept across the screen.

"Plate tectonics!" George recognized that map. He and Ben had learned that these plates were large masses of crust that came together like a puzzle to form the earth.

They had made a clay model of the world's tectonic plates a few months earlier.

"I don't think we saw this plate here," Ben pointed out—from a safe distance. He was concerned about the heat coming from the map.

"I know," George said softly, studying it further. "There's a lot we don't know, Ben."

"I wish my Dad were here," Ben gulped sadly. His Dad loved geology and he would be blown away by the accuracy of these maps.

Finally, the King pressed another gemstone to bring up climate conditions. Warm and cool air symbols revealed melting and cooling patterns of ice and snow.

"As you may know," he continued, "Volcanic eruptions warm up the earth. But there are other sources of heating that are doing the same thing—manmade sources. If the earth overheats, it could melt some of the glacier ice sheets that hold the tectonic plates in place. That could cause more earthquakes, tsunamis and more volcanic eruptions—ones that the fiery salamanders had not intended to move until much later in time."

"Fiery salamanders!" the boys interrupted.

The King pressed another gemstone. The screen changed to multiple screens revealing dragon-like creatures racing along magma deep under the earth's crust.

They were equipped with internal temperature sensors and an intuitive understanding of the global magma system and how to govern its movement.

"Wow," sighed Ben.

"I know," agreed George. "It's almost too much to absorb at one time."

"What," Ben stopped and pointed to sparkly points across the screen, "What are those little lights?"

"Come," the High King motioned them to the next wall. "I'll show you."

Chapter 26

The Earth Kingdom

The twinkling lights shone again on the western wall with great brilliance and luminosity. On this map, however, the lights were of many colors and large veins of gold and silver glittered across the screen.

"This is the Earth Kingdom, of which I am High King," the old gnome announced proudly.

"What are the different colors for?" George asked.

"Each color represents a certain type of mineral, or combination. That's why there are so many colors: sapphires, rubies, tourmalines, jade, and many more. The earth's minerals are vast in number."

The boys saw glittering on land and under water.

"That is gold," said the King as he pointed to the golden veins. "This is silver. That is copper. And there's more—each has a slightly different color. See?"

The metallic veins ran through the earth like the waterways on the northern wall map.

"There's dark brown here and here… and here," observed Ben. Layers of rock were mapped throughout the world, and between them were large dark brown pockets.

"Yes, those are compartments of oil that are stored under ground," he explained. "Mankind uses it as an energy source, but we value it for other reasons."

"You mean the drills that pull oil from the ground take it from these pockets?" Ben asked.

"Yes, they do, I remember now," George offered, "we saw a bunch of them when we were on vacation in Texas. Remember?"

"Oh, yeah," Ben nodded.

"Little do men know that by removing them from these storage areas, they are upsetting a balance in the earth below."
He sighed, "It takes thousands of years to create that oil, and they can drain a whole oil bed in less than one year."

He pressed another gemstone.

The screen lit up so brightly, George and Ben had to shield their eyes. The gnome turned the gemstone to the right, which lowered the intensity.

They looked again and blinked.

Huge crystalline structures were located in four areas on the globe. Their light was interconnected, also connecting to smaller crystals that, as a whole, formed a grid structure of light beams around the earth.

"This looks like lasers," Ben commented.

"You're partly right," the King agreed, "although mankind has not perfected that science to this degree. These crystals produce a sort of energy. They are very important. They keep many of our life systems and kingdoms alive."

The gnome was silent for a moment.

"Now, we come to the reason you are here."

Chapter 27

The New Kingdom

He brought the boys over to the main table. Sitting down at the table made Ben think of food. His stomach started to hurt. "I'm hungry," he said suddenly.

"I don't have the backpacks of food, Ben." George answered. "I left them downstairs."

"No matter," said the High King. He clapped his hands and soon an old gnome appeared at the door with refreshments. A platter of roasted nuts and seeds with a honey drink was quickly served.

The king dabbed his mouth with a napkin and continued. He touched a gemstone on the side of the table and a holographic image of the world—a complete globe—appeared before them all.

"All the elements of fire, air, water, earth and metal are made up of 97 natural elements."

He touched another gemstone.

The globe disappeared and a periodic table assembled in its place. The boys had studied basic chemistry, and had memorized the first 50 or 60 elements by heart. There were 119 elements on their table, and they were working their way up— to memorize them all.

"Why doesn't your table have all 119 elements," George asked.

The King grimaced.

"It is because we do not recognize the new elements—they are synthetic elements. They're manmade through unnatural tampering with the laws of chemistry… and they have wreaked havoc on the earth since their creation."

"In the year 1940, long before even your fathers were born, the world of man created its first synthetic element: Neptunium.

The forces of darkness, of anti-matter and anti-nature, were working closely with these scientists through mental urging and dark inspiration. Although the scientists believed they were thinking independent thoughts, it was the dark lords of anti-matter that had sent the ideas to them."

He stood up and put his hands on his hips. "The laws of Nature insist that we not influence one another through our thoughts—that is mental invasion!" he shouted.

When he saw that George and Ben were both surprised, he sat down, "When the first synthetic element was produced, they gloried in its achievement."

"Gentlemen," he looked at both boys, "there are four walls here, with four natural elemental kingdoms. But in truth, since that momentous day in 1940, there are now five kingdoms—the last is one that is most unnatural and unforgiving."

He shook his head and pressed another gemstone on the table.

"It is the Chemical Kingdom," he said sadly.

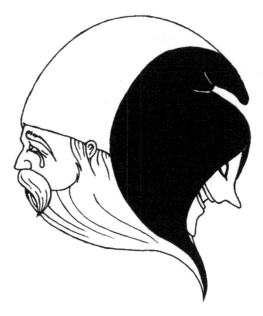

Chapter 28

The Wizards of Darkness

The children looked at the newly formed holographic globe in the center of the table. Black, red, grey and yellow chemical elements encircled the world—mixing with water, earth, air, and the plant and animal life that depended upon them.

"This is the evil I warned you of," he said as he touched the last gemstone.

The holograph in the middle of the table disappeared. The boys looked at the table surface—it had become a screen. But what it depicted, they couldn't even guess. It was completely black.

"What are we looking at?" Ben searched to find something he could recognize in the darkness on the table.

The High King sighed.

"That's just it, all elemental kingdoms have beings that govern and guide it. The Chemical Kingdom is guided by the Wizards of Darkness. We cannot see them. We can only see their destruction. We can hear evil thoughts—and that is their way of trying to influence us to go against nature and do bad deeds."

He pushed his chair away from the table.

"That is how they were able to influence all the gnomes on earth to leave their homes, reveal the earth's mineral treasures and submit to them."

Tears ran down his face as he walked over to the western wall once more. He touched a gemstone at the bottom of the screen. Gnomes by the thousands were hauling great loads of gems and mineral riches in carts upon carts.

The King wiped his eyes and tried to gain composure. "These are my people."

Young and old, male and female, gnomes were shackled to walkways to work in mines around the world. "Tap, tap, tap…" their pick axes broke the crystals down into smaller pieces.

"Tap, tap, tap."

"Wait," said Ben absentmindedly. "What does that sound like?"

He listened and thought again, "It sounds like…" he looked at George.

"Tiny spoons!" they said together.

"We heard this sound in our backyard!" Ben explained.

"Yes. There are mines deep below the ground—under mountains, fields, deserts and jungles. At this time the Wizards of Darkness have control over all of the minerals. The earth's treasures are being mined. The dark forces are trying to break down the grid of light."

"They depend upon the chemicals and want to add them to our water and air. They have convinced mankind to create unnatural products, such as plastics, using chemicals. They know it will filter into the other elemental kingdoms and change them."

"Their goal is to rule over all the kingdoms—and man."

Chapter 29

Riches

The boys sat in silence for a moment. "You said that all the elemental kingdoms are contacting men to help," George said.

"Who is helping? How can any of us turn this around?"

"We need many people to help because the Wizards of Darkness are attacking us from so many directions… water, air, and the slavery of the entire gnome kingdoms.

"The sylphs and undines have had to do all the work. They have contacted men and women they knew as children who are now powerful people. The sylphs need toxic air pollution to stop. The undines need mankind to know what they are doing to the world's water supply."

"But," he looked toward the western wall, "no one has been able to find a solution as to how to save the gnomes. If we tell mankind about the gnomes, they will also find out about our treasures. Once we save the gnomes, greed could make men take those riches for themselves."

He looked Benjamin and George squarely in their eyes.

"There are billions and billions of man dollars worth of gold and gems in our treasure stores. If you had possession of even a tiny bit of it, you could be rich beyond your wildest dreams."

The boys' eyes grew wide.

"Could you handle that type of pressure? Could you help us, restore the gnomes to our riches, and just walk away without anything?" he asked pointedly.

The boys were quiet once again.

"Ah-ha! That is why we contacted your fathers. We know that they have the integrity to help us without return or reward. As I say, they helped us before and refused gold and riches in payment for their services…"

He looked at them again, "…but human babies?!"

He half-scowled, with a hidden smile underneath, "Bah! It looks like we'll have to make due."

"Hey!" protested Ben.

"Yeah," added George. "We can help you without reward."

"Really?" the gnome asked, "You think so?"

"Yes!" they said together.

George continued, "My Dad says that we should do good things because good is…"

Ben joined in, "good to do!"

Ben smiled, "Yes, my Dad says that, too."

"Alright," the King nodded.

"I will accept your help. Firstly, because you have been raised well. I can see your fathers' goodness and spirit in you both. Secondly, because we need to move fast and I can see that you have great courage and good minds.

"Thirdly," he paused, "…because I have no other choice."

Chapter 30

Lizards

The old gnome entered once more, this time without the tray.

"I'm sorry, your Highness. An impulse just came in from The Fire Kingdom. You may wish to communicate with His Royal Highness the High Fire King privately."

"Yes, Bernard," King Hendrick replied. "Can you please show the boys back downstairs?"

"Of course," Bernard bowed.

He looked at George and Ben, "Please follow me."

They walked behind him down the long circular stairs…
very s-l-o-w-l-y. Ben tried not to giggle as they put one foot in
front of the other, in slow motion.

"This is what happens when you are ordered to follow an elderly
gnome!" he thought to himself. George looked up and caught
his glance. They shared a smile.

Once in the main living room, they found Mary sitting on the
couch, fully awake, talking to the Queen over butternut soup
and tea.

"Oh, you're back!" she cried. "Queen Fiona has told me that all
the gnome children and their families have been captured.
We must go and get them back!"

The two boys thought about what the King had said. It was
true—they had needed a technical read-out on the situation
before joining in. All Mary needed to know to get ready is that
gnome babies were in danger!

The good Queen offered the boys more nourishment and they
were grateful. "Now, you need to rest," she said as she led the
children to a small room full of pillows. "We are expecting
guests, but they will not be here for a few more hours. The
trees are refusing to shelter them, so they have decided to travel
through the night using other means."

The Queen placed a bell on a cushioned wooden stool by the
door. "Please feel free to ring if you need anything," she said
kindly. Then, she left the room.

Mary ran and hugged the boys. She had missed them.

"The Queen said that you went to some type of communication center at the top of the tree. What did you see?"

The boys could hardly explain everything they saw, but they did their best—for themselves as well as for Mary. They did not want to forget a thing.

They told Mary about the four elemental kingdoms, the gnomes, sylphs, undines, fiery salamanders, and the Wizards of Darkness.

When they had finished their tale, they all felt somber until Mary asked innocently, "So where do we find the Lizards of Darkness?"

The boys laughed until their stomachs hurt.

"No, Mary," Ben kindly correctly, "they are Wizards of Darkness." He couldn't help smiling.

"Oh!" Mary replied, deep in thought.

The boys finally recovered and settled in to rest.

Their tummies were full. The room was small, warm and snug. The pillows were soft and fluffy. The air was full of an aromatic woody scent. Soon, they all fell asleep.

Chapter 31

The Guests

The children awoke to laughter from the living room. Mary rubbed her eyes. She flattened her sweater, adjusted her hair bands and stepped lightly into the room. A small party of gnomes were sitting around the table, talking and laughing.

"Well, there you are," smiled the High King.

George and Ben joined them.

The High King stood up, as did the rest.

"This is Gottfried," he said as he pointed to an elderly gnome clad with blue clothing, and a grey vest. He had a light grey beard and spectacles.

"My great pleasure, children of man" bowed Gottfried. His

English had a strong German accent.

"And I am Jacob," a young gnome moved toward them holding out his hand to shake Ben's hand.

"I'm going to guard you on your journey," he said with a British accent. Then he winked at Mary, "Don't worry, fair maiden, I shall fight to defend you to the end!" He patted his gleaming sword case. He stood apart from the others in a bright red outfit.

"Ahem." A tall, young, and apparently shy gnome stood behind him, waiting to be introduced. He was hoping that Jacob would turn and introduce him. The tall gnome was afraid of man and he wasn't sure if he would be able to speak.

Jacob, however, was oblivious to the need for an introduction to his friend. He stood smiling at George, Ben and Mary. He was sure that they were very happy to meet him.

"Ahem," his friend repeated. Jacob heard it but still did not take the hint.

The High King stepped in, "Yes, well, now that the other introductions have been made," he said sternly while looking at Jacob, "I'd like to introduce you also to Vincent. He is from China."

Vincent was dressed in brown. He had a book in his hand, and was relieved that it prevented him from having to walk forward to shake anyone's hand. He bowed low to the children, not knowing what to say.

"Please join us," Gottfried bcekoned the children to sit down.

"We were just telling the king of our journey here. We had to use an alternate mode of travel."

The other gnomes laughed as he said the word 'alternate.'

The children politely listened.

"You see, those blasted trees are so intimidated by the Wizards that they have refused to grant us safe passage. So, Jacob traveled down to the earth's mantle to enlist help from the salamanders. Well, he convinced two fiery salamanders to carry us. They transported us from different corners of the world, above the oceans, well above the mountains, but when we reached the Great Forest, we could see the hoot owls, under the Wizards' spell, waiting to pluck us from the air."

"So, I led the salamanders underground through the mushroom system," Jacob interrupted.

"Gottfried rode one and Vincent and I the other. You should have seen those trees jump out of the ground as the fiery salamanders snorted fire. We singed their roots as we passed by!"

The gnome men laughed.

Queen Fiona had since entered the room.

"Shame on you, Jacob," she admonished. "Those trees are scared out of their wits already. Do not fault them for not helping us. They know that the gnomes are gone. They think that they might be next!"

Jacob looked thoroughly corrected. "My apologies, my lady," he said and bowed low.

"Hendrick," the Queen said, "you don't have much time. Allow Mary and I to prepare the packs while you meet to discuss your plans."

"Quite right, my dear," King Hendrick said as he rose. The gnomes and the boys quickly ascended the stairs and situated themselves around the central table.

Chapter 32

Crystal Mining

"Now we can speak plainly," The High King began.

George and Ben looked at each other from across the main table as if to give each other courage to continue.

"Before your arrival, I spoke to the High Fire King. There are a few developments," he said as he pressed a gemstone at the side of the table.

The South wall made a bell-like sound and its screen revealed the tectonic plates. Digital numbers flashed across the screen.

"The plates are shifting, resulting in higher volcanic activity just this week. As you can see from the numbers, the earth itself is shifting slightly—although those of us located on the center of those plates may not feel it."

"The mining of the crystals is harming the planet. We need to stop it now."

"How much damage has been done so far, your Highness," Gottfried asked.

The High King pressed a gemstone and the west wall screen lit up. "Here is the state of our crystals last year," he said as the crystals shone from different areas of the world. He turned the brightness down so that all could see.

"Here is the current state of our crystals." The screen changed to reveal the four large crystal shards still intact deep beneath the earth's surface, but the smaller ones were all but gone.

"It's a good thing that only the small ones are affected," sighed George.

The High King explained, "These may be tiny dots on a world map, but in reality they are large deposits that take up many miles of underground earth."

He picked one point on the map and zoomed in. The small point became larger and larger until a huge crystalline cave appeared on the screen. It was brilliant with light from every direction—all surfaces sparked.

He touched another gemstone and live video began. The cave was now dark, but for the lanterns of the gnomes who were mining the last remnants of crystal that remained. Then, he turned it off.

The High King began. "I have asked Gottfried and Vincent to come because of their knowledge of crystal energy. When their families became enslaved, Gottfried went into hiding with the Bavarian sylphs and Vincent with the undines in the Yangtze River. Now we are together," he smiled at the gnome men.

"From our different places in the world, we all have seen different ways that the Wizards of Darkness work. The dark forces are monitoring our communications. It is only safe to share what we know within the confines of the safe houses—like this tree."

"Why haven't the Wizards of Darkness mined the larger crystals?" Ben asked thoughtfully.

All the gnomes looked at each other.

Chapter 33

Crystal Energy

"Those crystals defend themselves," Vincent spoke up. The shy gnome continued, "They soak up and store the sun's energy. Mankind now uses silicon crystals to do the same thing on a smaller scale. Crystals are being used in much of your technology—computers, solar panels, all new technology depends upon them."

He shyly looked up at Ben and George, "These large crystals have been in the earth for millions of years. No one can mine them because, well…"

"No one can even touch them!" Jacob inserted. "They are so powerful, if anyone touched them, they would die on the spot."

Ben's eyes were wide. George winced at the thought of it.

"Sorry to say it so, but there it is," Jacob said as he folded his arms in front of him.

"Silicon crystals," Ben said as he thought back to his chemistry table. "Silicon has the atomic number of 14. Right, George?"

"Right," George replied. "So it would be natural, not from the chemical kingdom.

"Yes," Gottfried inserted, "but scientists that work for the Wizards of Darkness mine it in large quantities and change it to other things through a chemical process. Their scientists are working overtime to develop an element that will store the Sun's energy—something all elementals see as sacred."

He scowled, "Oh, there's nothing they will not do. They have no reverence for life. They would not use the Sun's energy to fuel life. They would only use it for destruction and harm."

Gottfried stood. "Your Highness, there is something strange that we noticed. In the days before the gnomes of Eastern and Western Europe were taken, the light from our crystal energy source grew dim. The underground bright lights had kept our spirits high and filled us with life. When it dimmed, I kept shaking off sad thoughts and then went into deep silence."

He paused for a moment. "Then, after several days of darkness, hundreds of gnomes vanished—entire families gone, young and old. I live alone, so I did not notice right away."

Vincent nodded, then spoke. "Your Highness, I was working on a new formulation that could bring ecological balance back to areas that had lost their oil stores. I'd been reading research books intently for weeks. The lights had dimmed, so I lit candles to continue reading. I came upon a great discovery. I ran to share it with the elders and saw that all the gnomes had vanished."

"The light dimmed," High King Hendrick repeated, stood up and walked over to the western wall. He scanned the data, but there were no records matching any reduction of crystal function.

"The Wizards must have technology that blocks out the crystals' energy," he said.

"...Or, your Highness," Vincent respectfully interrupted, "they might be using it."

"Stealing it, to be more exact," quipped Jacob.

"Yes," Vincent continued. "They could be using it to power mind control instruments. My grandfather used to say that just as the moon reflects the light of the sun to light up the night, Darkness cannot create its own power. It needs to use the energy of the Light. Maybe this is why they need the crystals in the first place—not for wealth..."

He paused, "...but for power."

"Your grandfather put it rightly, son," smiled the King. "We must know our enemies in order to defeat them.

We have some things that the chemical kingdom—try as they might— cannot create on their own: Light, Happiness, Goodness and a Higher Purpose. These are our true strengths and will help us restore balance to the Earth."

Ben and George looked a little blank.

The High King pointed at the eldermost gnome, "Gottfried's mind fought off the Wizards of Darkness' dark thoughts by 'shaking them off,' replacing them with higher, more positive ones."

Then, he gestured toward Vincent. "Vincent was not effected at all. This is because his mind was full of other thoughts— productive research, focusing on how to do good in the world."

"We must be vigilant," the king said as the others nodded in agreement. "As we approach the mining communities, we will surely encounter the thoughts of darkness. We must maintain powerful positive thoughts. But we won't be doing it alone...

"We have help."

Chapter 34

Muffins

Mary took the food out of the children's backpacks and repacked it. As she brought each piece out, Queen Fiona and the three fairies in the kitchen came to see. Food prepared by man was quite different from gnome cuisine. They smiled at each other with a strange recognition as they rewrapped the muffins and other goodies.

"Aw, feels like old times, does it not, Your Highness," remarked Nanna, the head cook.

"Yes, I almost forgot what a good cook Edna is," then she stopped and put her hand over her mouth.

She looked at Mary.

"You mean to say that you know Grandma McGillicutty?" Mary exclaimed.

A blush rushed to the Queen's cheeks. "Well, we know her, of course," she smiled as the others giggled. "But she does not know us, I'm afraid."

"You see, it all started years ago. One of our gnomes was tending to the earth near your house when he came upon the smell of a pie or a cake or some other sweet thing. He could not resist the smell. So, the story goes that he crept closer and was caught by two young boys!"

"Daddy and Uncle Jeffrey!" Mary clasped her hands together.

"Yes, quite so," the Queen nodded, "When the King heard, he was very alarmed because this particular gnome was our son, Caleb, you see."

She smiled. "The High King himself went to fetch him, with his finest men. When he found him, he saw that Caleb was very well taken care of—having had his fill of cakes and candies and chocolates. The boys had made a house for him. They treated him like a royal pet."

She giggled, "He almost did not wish to leave!"

"But King Hendrick soon put everyone in their places—gnomes were gnomes and 'human babies' were 'human babies,' he said."

It was a few months after that incident that we discovered that our forests were about to be bulldozed. The boys were called upon for help and they were able to work with grown-ups to declare The Great Forest a national wildlife sanctuary. They were very brave for their age.

She smiled at Mary. "And for many years our son went back to visit with them. He always brought back a little bit of something for us from Edna McGillicutty's kitchen."

They finished tying the bags of food and placed them back in the backpacks. Six backpacks of varying sizes were lined up by the door.

"There are only six backpacks," Mary observed. "Who is going?"

The Queen looked at her kindly, "Gnome Gottfried, Gnome Vincent, Gnome Jacob, George, Ben, and you."

"Isn't the High King going?" Mary questioned.

"No, dear," the Queen put her hand on Mary's arm. "He needs to be here to communicate with you and the rest of the elemental kingdoms. But, don't worry. We'll be watching your steps from the Great Room above. And you will, once again, be escorted by creatures that are determined to defy the Wizards of Darkness."

"Listen," she tilted her head, "the men are descending. It's time to go."

Chapter 35

Through the Tunnels

Mary ran out to greet Ben and George. She put her jacket on after handing the boys their outerwear. The gnome men placed the backpacks on the children and each other. They were ready. The High King placed his hands on the Ben and George's shoulders.

"Now, remember the plan," he said. Jacob will be leading the way. Send the doves back with messages."

"Yes, Your Highness," Ben said. "We will," added George.

"Very well," he said. He patted the backs of the other gnomes and stepped back toward Mary.

"Listen to the others, Mary," he looked at her seriously, "and take care not to be afraid as the Wizards will sense it. You can do it."

Mary nodded.

"Very well," he said, and opened the doors at the side of the tree.

Outside, Jacob pulled apart the lowest tree boughs to reveal hundreds of white-tailed deer waiting for their orders.

Jacob signaled for two deer to approach Ben and George to give each a ride. But before the boys could mount, they had to help Mary and the gnomes climb atop their own deer. Then, they held onto the neck of their deer and swung their legs around. The weight of their backpacks wobbled back and forth, and then they were steady.

With one signal from Jacob, off they rode, with deer to the front, deer to the back, and deer on either side. Mary put her head down low and held onto her deer's neck tightly.

Ben looked around cautiously to make sure that they were safe. He looked across to George and found that he was doing the same.

They rode to the edge of the forest and then turned into a familiar cave. It was the tunnel they came to the great forest in! As they dashed inside, some of the deer stayed behind. The hooves beating atop the soil inside the tunnel were light and silent—they had chosen their transportation well.

They rode through the tunnels for a very long time. It was dark, and the children had to trust that the deer knew where they were going. They finally reached a place where a light glow filled the caves. The deer slowed to a timid walk. They could see a faint outline of Jacob, up ahead. He put his finger over his mouth.

The light grew brighter and they came upon two paths—one toward the light, and one which veered away from it. Jacob signaled for them to go to the one that veered away. They went down this path and soon found themselves in darkness once again.

Jacob made a sound, which stopped the deer gently. He jumped off his deer and whispered to the others to stay still for a moment while he made preparations. They heard scuffling and some light sounds of metal, and then Jacob spoke.

"Okay. I will bring each of you to a tent I made—one by one. Wait for me to come to you." Mary felt hands carefully help her slide down off the deer. She followed the sound of Jacob's footsteps, then saw a flash of light as a tent flap lifted. She went inside and waited for the rest.

Soon, Ben and George joined her, followed by Gottfried and Vincent. They looked around them. The tent material was made of a thick fabric—something they had not seen before. Ben removed his magnifying glass. He could not see any visible fibers.

"Remarkable," he sighed.

Finally, Jacob returned. "The deer are no longer needed. I have thanked them. The rest is up to us."

"There are some bats standing by, but as you know, if or when we do need their assistance, it will have to be only in case of an emergency. Due to their need for echolocation, they are not very quiet."

Everyone smiled.

Chapter 36

The Rescue Mission

Gottfried turned to Jacob and said, "Well done, lad. You got us here safe and sound. Now it is time to set up what we need for our plan." "Right-e-o," Jacob agreed.

Gottfried continued, "This tent will serve us well for a base station. It is lightproof and soundproof. Let us set up our food and rest areas. Young miss," he turned to face Mary, "may we put you in charge of that?"

"Yes!" answered Mary. She knew where the food was stored. She made sure that each person had emergency food in their jackets and placed the rest in a little corner to be used as a makeshift pantry.

"We need a map center, too," offered Vincent. He took a folded tunnel map from his backpack. Ben unhooked his telescope case and pulled out his maps, too.

"Good," surveyed Gottfried.

"Now, remember, our mission is to go straight to the mine, observe the gnomes, discover any weaknesses in their captivity, and note them. We are not to make contact unless they seek us. Then we must be very discreet."

Vincent explained to Mary, "If we find a way to free the gnomes in this mine, then we can go back to the High King and he will make a request for all kingdoms to launch a rescue in every mine across the globe—simultaneously."

Gottfried, then took out a thin bark-covered plate with three gemstones upon it: an orange topaz, a green emerald and a deep purple amethyst. A golden wire wrapped around each stone and connected them in fancy curls.

"This," he announced to all watching, "is our communication device. We'll be able to send messages to High King Hendrick through it."

"But, how?" Ben asked as he studied the curious object.

"It looks more like a big clunky piece of jewelry," George added. "Oh, and it's so beautiful!" Mary exclaimed, clasping her hands together in the secret wish that it might be something she could keep.

"Oh no, quite the opposite," Gottfried continued.

He reached inside his vest and took out a headphone piece. He touched the end of the wire to the topaz. It began to glow.

The children gasped in astonishment.

Next, out of the other pocket, came a small conch shell. This, the elderly gnome placed between the amethyst and emerald. They began to glow, too.

"Hello?" came a small voice from the headphones in Gottfried's hand.

"Hello, your Highness," Gottfried said as he spoke directly into the shell. "I am happy to report that we have arrived."

"Very well," High King Hendrick replied. "You know what to do. I'll await your next communication. May the Light of all Creation be with you."

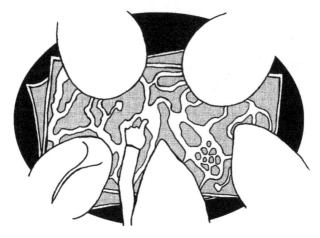

Chapter 37

The Crystal Mine

Gottfried placed the headphones and shell by the gem board.

"What did the King mean... 'You know what to do'?" George asked as he looked up at Gottfried.

"Well, for now we will study the process of the mining of the crystals and see if we can discover their weaknesses and their strengths," Gottfried said as he studied a map. He looked determined to find a good place to observe the mining.

Vincent and Jacob joined him, looking to mark the places where they could oversee operations without being spotted.

Mary began to yawn while putting the last of the food away.

"You can't be tired, now, Mary," Ben teased. "How can you be tired when we're about to scout out the mine?"
"It's too exciting to miss!" George added.

"I know," Mary yawned again. "But it was a long journey from the Great Tree and I'm sleepy."

Ben quickly made a bed for her. They bade her goodnight and she soon fell asleep.

Finally, Gottfried quietly outlined the plan.

"The mine is here," he pointed to a place on the map that wasn't too far away from their house and the hidden room under the shed.

"And we are here," he pointed to a place on the other side of the map. "So, we will have to go back through this southern tunnel that opens up at several points along the mining cave wall."

Vincent continued, "The holes in the wall are large. I'm not sure how we will cross them without being seen..."

He stopped suddenly when Gottfried pointed at another spot on the map, "What is there?"

"Where?" asked Ben. He leaned in to see another system of tunnels at the top of the page.

"It's an old tunnel that will lead us right toward the north side of the crystal cave!" Gottfried replied.

"Yes, but look here," Jacob put his finger on what looked to be an entrance to the cave leading from that tunnel. He shook his head. "It's the only way in and out from this side, so, chances are, it will be very heavily guarded."

"The exposed holes in the tunnel are looking better every minute," Vincent whispered.

Gottfried was quiet.

He rubbed his bearded chin.

"I believe it might be wise to send out two teams—Vincent and George to the South and Jacob and Ben to the North."

"But, what if we come across trouble?" Ben asked. "What do we do then?"

Jacob and Vincent looked at each other knowingly.

"That's why we each need one of you to come with us," Vincent shyly responded. "You are our secret defense system."

"Us?!" The boys were surprised.

"Yes," Gottfried smiled. "The Wizards of Darkness cannot harm the sons of Man directly. As elementals, we are vulnerable. But if you use your thoughts to shield us…"

"You mean like think of light around us or something?" George interrupted.

"Just so, son," Gottfried looked up at the boys.

He continued, "…then, we can complete our work quickly, undisturbed."

He looked kindly upon sleeping Mary. "And I shall stay here to watch over your sister and maintain open lines of communication."

"Time to go," said Vincent.

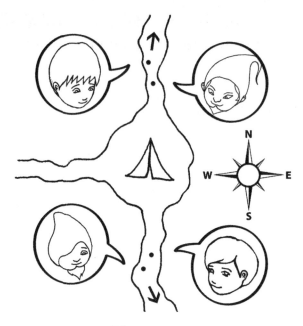

Chapter 38

Scouting

Vincent put his pack on and nodded at George. George grabbed his jacket and followed him quietly out the door.
A moment later he lifted the flap and poked his head back in.

"Be safe, Ben." He said with a creak in his voice.

"Okay," said Ben.

"Oh, he'll be safe!" Jacob protested. "He'll be with me!"

"Okay," George said and he quickly left to catch up with Vincent.

Ben put his jacket on and checked his pockets for food.

He felt his flashlight in his pocket. He looked at Jacob who was busy collecting various items for his own pack.

Jacob lifted the flap and said, "Come on, Ben. We have to go now."

The tunnel was pitch black. Ben heard the soft scuffling sound of Jacob's feet ahead of him and carefully followed. They walked for what seemed like a very long time before they started to see a soft glow ahead. Soon, they heard muffled tapping sounds. Ben suddenly realized that it was the same sound he had heard when lying down in the backyard of the house.

Tap. Tap. Tap.

The taps grew louder and sharper as the light grew brighter. Soon, Ben could see Jacob clearly before him, and he signaled to Ben to walk slowly and quietly, next to the tunnel wall. Up ahead was a great, wide opening. It was the main entrance of the mining cave that was pictured at the north side of the map. Now, they could hear voices. They stopped.

Jacob motioned to Ben to come nearer. He softly whispered, "Ben, you need to put up a shield now."

Ben looked at him quizzically, "I don't know how."

Jacob had been staring ahead to figure out their next steps, but this comment made him stop.

He gazed at Ben, "You mean, you don't know how to use your power?"

"No," Ben answered, "Gottfried said something about helping by using our thoughts, but I don't know how. George and I have never done it before."

Jacob looked down for a moment, deep in thought.

"This is serious, Ben," he finally whispered. "I don't know, either, because only the sons of Man can do it. We cannot."

Ben thought for a moment. Then, a memory flooded in from a bedtime story his father used to tell him. He told of how two little boys passed through a scary forest full of wolves by creating a force field of some sort.

'Think, think, think,' Ben said to himself. 'How did they do it?' Suddenly an image came.

He saw the boys visualizing light around them—keeping their minds focused on seeing a bright wall of light moving through the forest with them. They thought of nothing else. By the time they reached the other side of the forest, they had safely passed the wolves. They were in full view of them, but were able to pass completely unnoticed.

'That's it!' he realized.

Ben closed his eyes and thought of light. He saw light shining all around him, glowing brighter and brighter. He opened his eyes and looked at Jacob. Jacob seemed to look through him and seemed worried. He stopped visualizing the light.

Jacob gasped as Ben rematerialized in front of him.

"That's it!" he excitedly whispered. "You just did it!"

"Now," he continued quietly, "can you do that for me, too?"

Ben closed his eyes and saw a light wall around both he and Jacob. He held that vision for a minute, and then opened his eyes.

"Did it work?" he asked.

"I'm not sure," Jacob replied. "I could see you the whole time."

Chapter 39

To the South

Vincent and George had journeyed through damp, dark tunnels for what seemed like hours.

"Rrrrr…" George's stomach growled.

He patted his jacket and found a bump at the bottom of his pocket. He reached down and felt a soft cloth with something that felt bread-like within.

"Vincent?" he said as he pulled the parcel out.

"Yes…" Vincent quietly replied.

"Could we stop for a moment?" George asked.

"I have some food to share," he said. He felt the snack in his hand, he realized the shape was more of a muffin, although somewhat squashed by having been in his pocket.

Vincent's footsteps stopped.

George began to open up the wrapping, releasing a delicious smell of sweet pumpkin, maple and cinnamon.

Vincent's flashlight was on in a moment to fully reveal what was in his hands: a plump, hearty muffin. George broke it into halves and handed one to Vincent. They sat down to rest and eat. Vincent kept the flashlight under his jacket so that only a little bit of light escaped for their short meal.

"How much longer do we have to go before we're there?" George asked after finishing his half-muffin.

"That's just it," Vincent explained. "We're not sure how old the maps are… or how accurate. We'll just have to keep going until we see or hear something."

"Okay…" George dusted off his pants and stood up.

Vincent quickly flashed his light ahead and then turned it off.

"Ready?" he asked.

"Sure," George replied. They could hear each other's footsteps once more as they progressed further into the tunnel system. They used their right hands to feel the wall as they navigated forward.

Soon, Vincent stopped.

The wall had opened to the right. He flashed his light briefly to reveal two tunnels before them.

"What do we do?" asked George.

"I'm not sure," Vincent whispered. "This split isn't on the map." They stopped to think.

Tap. Tap. Tap.

There it was.

Tap. Tap. Tap.

It was faint, but tapping sounds could be heard in the silence.

"Can you hear that?" asked George.

"Yes, I can. But I'm not sure which tunnel it is coming from," Vincent said as he strained to listen.

"It's not coming from ahead," George thought out loud. "It is behind us... I think we might have missed a tunnel that went to the left."

Tap. Tap. Tap.

Vincent listened thoughtfully. "Yes, you are right. I wonder why we did not hear it before."

"Maybe they stopped for lunch," George joked, although he quickly realized that he might be right.

Vincent took his arm and steered him to the opposite tunnel wall and they changed course. They began to feel the wall back in the direction from which they came. The tapping grew louder and louder.

Soon, they felt an opening to another tunnel. Metal clanking reverberated through the opening. They walked inside the new tunnel, steadily getting closer to the mining sounds.

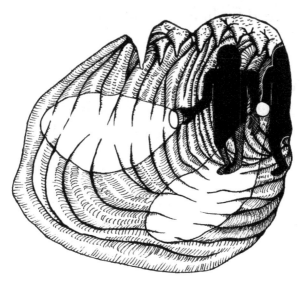

Chapter 40

To the North

"You could see me this time?" Ben whispered nervously to Jacob. He wasn't sure what he had done differently, except that this time he had visualized both he and Jacob in the Light.

"That's right. You didn't disappear," Jacob whispered back.

All of a sudden the voices they had heard before grew louder and they could hear footsteps coming their way. Lights started to flash in their direction.

"Try again," Jacob mouthed.

Ben closed his eyes and started to visualize walls of light around them. Jacob stood close to the wall. The tunnel lit up and two tall, dark figures soon appeared before them.

Ben disciplined himself not to look. He knew he had to stay focused on seeing light around both he and Jacob. He imagined the light was as bright as a wall of fire.

The dark figures flashed their lights in different directions as if they were looking for something.

"Yert trib yuhm," Ben heard one say to the other.

The flashlight shone directly at Jacob, but seemed to go straight through his little body. There wasn't even a shadow behind him.

'Light,' Ben said to himself as he continued his visualization.

"Nyahb," the other said in what seemed like an agreement to the other fellow's comment.

The light was directed toward Ben, then beyond him, and then they turned back and walked away.

Both Jacob and Ben held their breath until they could no longer hear the voices.

"You did it!" Jacob finally whispered. "I guess I could see you because you had cloaked us both in invisibility. Jolly good job."

Ben smiled.

"Now, you've got to do it again," Jacob said as he slowly led him closer to the cave entrance. "We need to have a look inside."

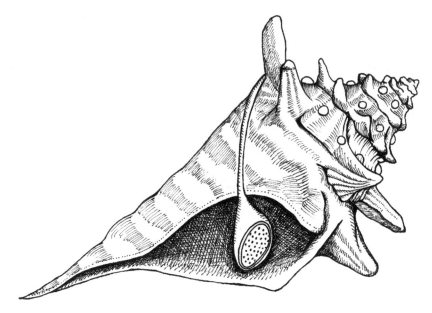

Chapter 41

Unexpected News

"Hello?" Mary heard as she opened her eyes from her nap.

"Hello?" High King Hendrick's voice was heard from the headphones by the gemboard.

"Hello, your Highness," Gottfried responded. "We're here."

Mary rubbed her eyes and stretched.

"Gottfried, something is showing up on the screen here. Something quite unexpected…" he hesitated. "Who is there with you?"

"Mary is here with me," Gottfried promptly replied.

"Any news from Jacob, Vincent and the boys?" Hendrick asked.

"Not yet, your Highness. They split up—Vincent and George to the South and Jacob and Ben to the North. We're not sure how long it will take for them to travel to the observation points and return, so we are waiting patiently."

"I see," King Hendrick seemed pensive. "Mary, can you hear me?"

"Yes, I can," Mary spoke up.

"Good," the king replied. "I need for you to be brave and to hear this most recent news knowing that we are doing everything we can to help."

He paused.

Mary and Gottfried looked at each other.

"In the past hour, we have seen glimpses of people in the mine—there are three men there. They seem to be, well, captured. Tied up. Now, Mary, I cannot say for sure, because you know that it has been a very long time since I saw both your father and your Uncle Jeffrey, but it seems to me that two of the men resemble them very much, indeed."

Mary's face instantly transformed to one of great worry. "Then, we've got to save them!" she declared emphatically.

"Yes," King Hendrick agreed.

Gottfried patted her shoulder. "But, we'll need your help to stay calm so that we can do just that," he said firmly. "We need our wits about us. Nothing will be served by becoming overly emotional. It will not serve them."

Mary swallowed hard.

"I understand," she said determinedly.

"Good," the High King continued. "Gottfried, you will not be able to send word to either group of this development. They will either discover it on their own, or will return with their observations and learn of it from you. I hope the latter is the case so that we have time to plan. I'm seeking help as we speak."

"But, Your Highness," Gottfried picked up the shell and began to speak quietly. "What will happen if the boys catch glimpse their fathers? They could easily lose their ability to proceed unrecognized…"

"Quite so," the King's voice sounded weak and small for a moment.

"Let us remain positive," the King spoke again, this time with hopeful strength.

"Mary, help Gottfried for now and trust that help is on its way. I do need to go now so that I can continue to arrange things from my end."

"Godspeed, your Highness," Gottfried bid the King.

Chapter 42

A Piggyback Ride

Tap. Tap. Tap. Chink.

Light was beginning to flood the tunnel. George and Vincent slowed their steps so that they would not be heard.

A dusty smoke filled the air and George pulled up his shirt around his mouth so that he could breath more easily. Vincent reached into his pocket for a handkerchief and did the same.

They followed a bend in the tunnel and suddenly came upon three or four holes in the wall where a brighter light was shining through. The holes ranged from basketball size and shape to long tall slits in the wall that were as high as the tunnel itself. Vincent carefully bent near the first hole and peered through.

He immediately pulled back. George held his breath.

Vincent's brow was furrowed. He pressed his hand to George's chest as if to say, 'don't come any closer.' Then, he looked into the hole again. This time, he watched for a long time.

Finally, he withdrew and took a notebook and pencil out of his pack. He began to draw a diagram, noting everything that he had seen.

George watched as Vincent scribbled vigorously. Details of the crystal mine began to come alive on the page. From what George could see, their tunnel was situated above the mine, looking down. Because of this, Vincent was able to survey the layout easily.

The mine was vast. Vincent marked several camps of gnomes that were in action. He drew pictures of various machinery, and sleeping quarters, and ended his drawing with a star on the far right corner of the page.

When he was done, he looked up at George and pointed back toward the cave. It was time to return.

George leaned forward to take a look before leaving, but Vincent kindly shook his head. He didn't want to take a chance to explain out loud. They needed to return to the tent quickly to give King Hendrick their news.

Back through the tunnel system they traveled. This time, George led the way and Vincent followed. George was a good tracker and had remembered the way well.

The tapping grew more faint as the tunnels grew dark and damp again. They kept up a fast pace on their return.

"Oh!" Vincent exclaimed long after they were in the dark. The taps could no longer be heard.

"Are you okay?" George asked. He couldn't see a thing. He started to feel around in his backpack for his own flashlight.

"I'm… okay," Vincent replied.

George turned on his light. Vincent was on the ground.

"I didn't see the depression on the floor. I think I might have twisted my ankle." Vincent's face was pain-ridden.

"That's okay," George said. "I give Mary piggyback rides all the time."

"Piggy-what?" Vincent looked very confused.

George motioned for him to get onto his back.

Once on, Vincent held onto the wall to guide them to their makeshift home base—the tent.

Chapter 43

Blueprints

Ben began to visualize light around the two of them, as Jacob moved forward.

Tap. Tap. Tap.

'Stay calm. Think of light.' Ben told himself.

Jacob was now entering the cave entrance, with Ben close behind. Ben kept his vision focused on the back of Jacob's heels so that he would not be distracted.

They walked right past the front guard—another tall figure that Ben was glad not to take notice of.

Jacob looked around him. Gnomes were everywhere. They were organized into small groups to mine the crystal caves at every point of each wall. There were strong young gnomes that picked at the wall, even younger gnomes who sorted the pieces, and elderly gnomes who broke large crystals into smaller ones.

There was a packaging area that was linked to some kind of transport rail system.

Tents and cots were placed within the cave at different points, presumably for meals and sleep. Although how anyone could sleep through the noise of a mine or the brightness of the cave, he wondered.

Then, something caught his eye. He looked back; to make sure that Ben was still behind him, then stepped forward.

Several tall guards were huddled around a table. As he looked at their faces, he gasped. They looked mechanical. They spoke to one another. They sounded like men. They were the same size as men. But, they were not real. They were looking at some papers on the table.

Jacob looked back at Ben again. 'Good lad,' he thought as he saw Ben's concentration.

He stepped toward the table to see if he could see between the nearest two figures. He could not. He moved around the table until he found an opening. There, on the table, lay a set of blueprints. Now, he could see what looked like people sitting at the table. Yes! They were men!

Each man was tied to a chair.

Although he did not understand the language of the guards, he could tell that they were not happy about something.

"Archin bok il bleg!" one guard said as he pointed to the blueprints.

"I will not tell you!" came the emphatic reply.

Ben looked up.

"Dad!"

Chapter 44

A Work Project

The tent flap waved open. Mary and Gottfried were relieved to see George and Vincent step through. It had been hours. Mary jumped up to hug George.

"You're hurt!" Mary exclaimed as she saw George set Vincent carefully down on a mat.

"It is not serious," Vincent said as he rolled up his pant leg, exposing a pink, swollen ankle.

Mary took the stuffed animals out of her bag and placed them under Vincent's foot to elevate it. Vincent politely received her attentions, while motioning to George to pass him his backpack.

"Here's the layout of the cave..." he began shyly as he opened his notebook.

"Did you see Daddy?" Mary interrupted. "Is he okay?"

"What?" George's face grew white.

Vincent looked at Gottfried. "I did see some men in the cave. They were being questioned."

Gottfried looked at George, "George, we received word from High King Hendrick that both your father and your uncle may be in the mine. He recognized them in video images received while you were in the tunnels."

George still looked stunned. He held Mary's hand as they looked at each other.

Gottfried continued, "We hoped that you would return without being noticed so that we could plan a rescue."

"But how could they be in the mine?" George knew it wasn't good.

His parents were supposed to be on an important business trip, a "work project" they called it. And his aunt and uncle were in the Himalayas.

It wasn't possible.

But, then again, none of this seemed possible, either.

"Wait," George stopped.

"Any news from Ben and Jacob? Do they know?"

Chapter 45

Captured

Jacob and Ben instantly appeared before the guards and the men at the table. Ben and his father shared a mixture of love, relief, and then a strong realization of the present danger.

The dark figures seized the gnome and boy. They pushed them toward the table.

"Don't touch him!" Ben's father demanded.

"Arcknad abat andan!" the main guard sneered.

Ben looked at his father.

"Archin bok il bleg!" the guard said as he pointed to the blueprints.

"No," he replied.

"Archin bok il bleg!" the guard screamed as he pointed again, this time at Ben.

Ben's father looked down at the ground in pain.

"Okay, okay..." he said softly.

The guards pushed Ben toward his father and Ben hugged him. Jacob was quickly bound to a nearby table leg.

The guards must not have seen Ben as a threat. They took the blueprints, and left the humans to themselves as they went to a series of block buildings in a dark corner of the cave, leaving one guard behind to stand watch.

"That must be their living quarters," Jacob quietly observed.

"No," Ben's uncle Brent replied. "It's a place they "plug in" to communicate with something they call the Wizards of Darkness."

"Are you okay, Ben?" his father looked at him.

Ben nodded.

"You shouldn't be here," he said seriously.

"Dad, never mind about me. What are you and Uncle Brent doing here?" Ben asked.

"Yes, and what do they want with those papers?" Jacob added.

"Oh…" the third man at the table began. "Those papers reveal the geographic infrastructure of a very important place."

"One of the main crystals?" Ben asked.

"He's met Hendrick, Jeffrey!" Uncle Brent exclaimed enthusiastically.

"Well," Ben's father looked at Ben more closely.

"Did you find us through the tunnels?" his uncle asked him.

"Yes," Ben nodded. "We all met King Hendrick and his wife first—George and Mary and I—before we came here."

"George and Mary? Where are they? Are they alright?" his uncle asked him.

"Yes, well, at least I think so… Mary is waiting for us in one of the tunnels. George and Vincent went to the southern part of the mine. Jacob and I traveled north."

By the looks on their faces, Ben could see that he had introduced names that they had not recognized.

"Oh, right," he said. "Dad, Uncle Brent, this is Jacob."

"Cheerio," Jacob smiled, "I'd shake your hand, but I'm a little tied up at the moment."

Laughter broke the tension around the table.

"As long as we are making introductions," Ben's father added,

"I am Jeffrey, this is my brother, Brent, and this is our colleague and mentor, Dr. Nathan Abraham."

"Nice to meet you," Jacob said as he looked at each of the men. Then, he became serious. He turned toward Ben.

"Young lad, this might be more difficult, but do you think you could disappear again, only this time with all five of us?"

Ben gulped.

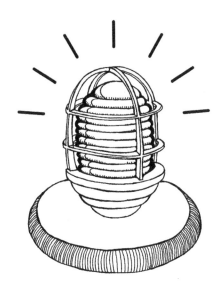

Chapter 46

S.O.S.

The gemboard lit up.

"There's a call, Gottfried!" Mary pointed to the shell.

"Hello!" came a tiny voice from the headphones, but the voice was not that of the High King.

"Hello?" Gottfried picked up the shell.

"Hello, Gottfried. It's Queen Fiona," she called out.

"King Hendrick has left. He is coming with reinforcements. He has asked me to ask you to please stay where you are. He is quite worried."

There was a strain in her voice.

"We can see from our monitor that Jacob and Ben are now with the three men in captivity. But we cannot see George or Vincent. Are they with you?"

"Yes, my Queen," Gottfried replied. "They are quite safe."

"That is a great relief," the Queen's voice wavered. "There is something else…"

"Yes, your Highness?" Gottfried asked.

"We've confirmed that the men were captured from the Tibetan region of China," she sighed.

"They were scientists who had been doing research on the crystal structures in that area. Recently, they came across of one of Earth's largest crystals, hidden deep within the Himalayas. They have maps containing the location."

"But, our Dad is a businessman," George offered, "How could he have been involved? Uncle Jeffrey is the geologist."

"I am not certain, George. But your father knows many things about the elemental world. If your uncle had come across something and needed help, I'm sure your father would be right there to help him. The Wizards of Darkness want those maps and would do anything to get them."

Beep-beep-beep. Beep-beep-beep.

"And speaking of that," she continued, "We just received an S.O.S."

Queen Fiona was quiet for a moment.

"Gottfried, there is an S.O.S. signal coming from within the tunnel system. It looks like it is coming from the old tunnel system that leads East."

Beep-beep-beep. Beep-beep-beep.

"It's King Hendrick. He needs help. Can you find him?" she sounded panicked.

"We'll do our best, your Highness." Gottfried looked over at Vincent who was already unrolling the maps to find the eastern tunnel system. George was looking over his shoulder, studying each twist and turn.

"It's close, my Queen. We'll leave now," Gottfried said as he nodded to George.

"Thank you," Queen Fiona replied.

Mary grabbed muffins and pushed them into George and Gottfried's pockets as they flew out of the tent.

Chapter 47

Now You See

Ben took a deep breath. He closed his eyes and imagined a great wall of light surrounding everyone around the table—his father, his uncle, their friend and Jacob.

"Ben?!" he heard his father cry out, "Where are you? What's happening?"

He opened his eyes.

"I'm right here," he blinked.

All three men looked at him in complete shock.

"I'm not sure it worked this time," Jacob exhaled softly. "This time you disappeared, but we did not."

"Oh," Ben looked disappointed.

"What do you mean: *this time*?" his father directed to Jacob, "You mean he's disappeared before?"

"Yes, Dad," Ben put his hand on his father's shoulder. "But, I thought you had prepared me for it. You know… from the story you used to tell me?"

"What story?" his father looked puzzled.

"The story about the boys in the forest… the one with the wolves."

"Oh," a realization came over his father's face. He looked at his brother across the table.

"High King Hendrick told us that story," Uncle Brent explained. "We never knew what it meant."

Ben's father nodded. "Yes, and there were other stories, too."

The men looked at each other, "They must all have secret meanings."

Ben's father gazed at Ben for a moment, "That means that you disappeared by visualizing light. Is that it?"

"Um, yeah," Ben began.

"Unbelievable," the quiet scientist, Dr. Abraham, remarked.

"But I stopped suddenly when I heard your voice. When I concentrate on light, I cannot see what is around me very clearly. When I heard you, I had to see you… to see if you were okay." He sniffed to hold back a tear.

"I understand, son," his father's eyes were moist as well.

"Ben," interrupted Jacob, "I wonder if…"

He lowered his voice considerably to a hushed whisper, "I wonder if you could do that again and lift the pocket knife from your pack to cut us free."

Ben closed his eyes immediately.

The men looked at each other calmly as Ben disappeared.

They began to casually talk amongst themselves while, one by one, their ropes were cut loose. The men continued to sit and talk as if nothing had happened. They kept their hands behind their chairs, as if still bound.

Ben reappeared quietly at the side of his father's chair.

The guard had not seen a thing.

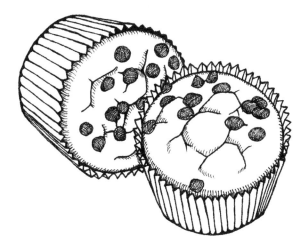

Chapter 48

Growling

George and Gottfried raced through the tunnels. At one point, George carried the stately gnome on his back in order to race faster. Gottfried's spirit could run faster than his short legs.

They finally entered a segment of the tunnels where the darkness lifted and a small amount of light came through, from within the cave, they surmised. George slowed down to a quiet pace so that they might not be heard. Gottfried held onto George's upper arms, guiding him this way and that by tugging on his right or left as he saw an upcoming turn.

They soon heard sounds up ahead.

It was a mixture of footprints, hoof prints and the fluttering of wings. George let Gottfried down and they crept closer.

Soon, a familiar voice bellowed out from the tunnels ahead.

"Unhand me and let my friends go!" King Hendrick bravely demanded.

A bend in the tunnel ahead revealed a brand new scene. George and Gottfried cautiously peered around the bend.

Scores of fairies lit up the room with a hazy light. They were trapped in what seemed like grey clouds, suspended in midair. Several gnomes and forest animals were surrounded by a fence of dark energy emitted from the hands of towering tall, dark figures.

George and Gottfried pulled back and looked at each other. "What can we do?" they seemed to say through their eyes.

George furrowed his brow and looked like he was about to get ready and jump in to fight. Gottfried calmly put his hand on his shoulder and shook his head. He held up his forefinger.

'Wait,' it seemed to say.

"Artchun klip ar har," one of the dark figures ordered. He kicked King Hendrick to make him move.

"Well, there certainly isn't any call for that!" the High King retorted.

Gottfried held George back.

"Artchun klip!" he said again as he moved the dark energy fences forward, forcing all beasts of land and air within to move along with it.

The other dark figures moved the clouds containing an army of trapped fairies inside slowly down the tunnel system. When they were far enough away, Gottfried signaled to George that they had better follow. Then, he stopped.

"Young George," he whispered as softly as he could. "It is time to use your thoughts to shield us. Do you remember the ancient ways of man?"

"It's strange, but I do know what you mean," George slowly realized that all the stories his father and uncle had told the boys at bedtime were real. He closed his eyes and saw a great wall of light around him.

Gottfried looked ahead as the human boy disappeared before his eyes. He was astonished. He knew that it was possible, but had never seen it done before. Before him was nothing but dark cave walls and damp ground.

"Rrrrr…"

George's stomach growled.

He instantly reappeared. He blinked at Gottfried with great embarrassment.

"I don't think this is going to work unless we refuel with muffins…" he smiled.

Gottfried did his best to hold back his laughter. George reached into his pocket and pulled out another safely kept muffin.

Chapter 49

Dignified Company

"Do you know your way back, Jacob?" Ben's father inquired. The men knew they had little time to escape, and the present moment, where only one guard was stationed, was an opportune one.

"I do," was the quick response.

"But the blueprints..." the scientist began.

"...Are replaceable," his uncle whispered. "Jeffrey knows the exact location, Nathan. Without him, the blueprints are meaningless."

The scientist nodded.

The table was quiet once more.

"Dad?" Ben broke the silence.

"Yes, Ben," his father's tone was weary, but warm.

"I'd like to try it again—with all of us," he replied. "But…"

"Yes?" his father looked at him directly.

"Well, if it's the sons of man who can do this, why can't you and Uncle Brent and Dr. Abraham help, too?"

The men exchanged quick glances.

"You're quite right," the old scientist softly agreed. "36 hours ago, if you had told me that gnomes were real, I would have thought that you were crazy. But, now, I'm ready to believe and do just about anything to get us out of here."

He smiled at Ben, "Tell us what we need to do, young man."

"Arch it trak un fredyurd!" the guard hollered.

They looked up, but found that he was not yelling at them, but toward a new group emerging from the cave entrance.

"Drak bhak lun poh gunglinh!" came the response from another guard. Behind him appeared cloud after cloud of contained smoke—grey energy that had slow-moving captives inside.

The prisoners began to fill one far section of the cave, as more and more captured creatures filed in. The mining gnomes took no notice and continued with their work, hypnotically, mechanically.

"Hands off, and stop kicking, for Heaven's sake!" they heard.

Ben and Jacob looked at each other. They knew that voice.

Soon deer, raccoons, otters, rabbits, squirrels, mice, and many types of winged birds began to appear in what seemed to be an electronic, moving grey mist.

"Now, this is quite enough. You certainly do not know who you are dealing with, young man, or, well, whatever you are!"

Before long, High King Hendrick emerged—rattled, but still quite dignified. He shook the dust from his arms and legs and adjusted his hat. He looked across the cave as if searching for something.

Then, he saw everyone at the table.

He immediately locked eyes with Ben, looked greatly relieved and gave him a reassuring wink.

They smiled at each other.

Chapter 50

Peek-a-Boo

"Artchun klip!" the guard shouted as he pushed the little king forward. The king stumbled and then found his way toward the table. He stood near Jacob and then looked up at the guard.

"I demand an explanation from the Wizards of Darkness! I demand to speak with them immediately," he pointed his finger at the guard's face.

The guard's mechanical face lit up as red digital data ran through some type of circuitry within his eyes.

High King Hendrick kept his terror in check as he stared above him, "I know that you can contact the Wizards who until now have been cowards, putting all elemental life into a trance-like state to do their bidding. No choice is involved, only terror and treachery. But, you cannot control me. And you cannot control my friends. Your day is done!"

He stamped his foot.

"Tell them that!"

More data processed within the guards eyes. Then, he tied the king to another table leg and walked away.

"Hello, Jeffrey," King Hendrick looked around the table.

"Hello, Brent," he continued.

"My, you boys have grown…" he teased.

A soft chuckle echoed across the table.

"Your Highness," Jacob nodded toward the scientist, "May I introduce to you Dr. Nathan Abraham, a scientist."

"Very honored, indeed," the king bowed his head as he realized that he could not shake his hand.

Dr. Abraham bowed in reply.

Jacob had been looking intently at King Hendrick, hoping to regain his attention without another word. He raised his eyebrows up and down.

The king sensed something and met his gaze.

Jacob wiggled his fingers quickly. The king realized that Jacob's ropes had been cut.

Then he felt a tug on the ropes that bound his own hands. They were cut away in an instant. As the king held his ropes in place, he looked around for Ben, who was nowhere to be seen. He slowly reappeared next to his father.

"Remarkable," King Hendrick said beneath his breath.

"We always believed in the old stories, but how wonderful it is to see that they are true… with our own eyes," he marveled.

"You mean, you didn't know that this was going to work before you sent us out here?!" George materialized at the far end of the table by Dr. Abraham.

A newly exposed Gottfried, who was right beside him, hastened to whisper, "George! Remember the light!"

They disappeared again.

The men were stunned.

They heard a few steps.

"Hi, Dad," George's voice whispered as he faintly appeared, grinning from ear to ear, and disappeared again.

George's father could not remove the oddest look from his face—a mixture of love, pride, and amusement all at once.

"Hi, George," he whispered back.

He felt a hug around his neck.

"I'm okay, son," his eyes watered.

"Everything is going to be okay."

Chapter 51

True Power

"Gottfried," the king whispered. "Both you and George must continue, as planned, to the gnomes. I know it seems dangerous, but more help is on its way, and we have to know if it works…"

"What works?" Dr. Abraham asked, leaning toward them.

"We need to free the gnomes from whatever dark spell they are under. The boys might be able to help by disturbing whatever thought waves are being used to control them. The force field they are able to create and maintain might just be our only hope."

"Hey!" George appeared suddenly, "I thought that you said that we were 'human babies' and not really able to help at first…"

He looked at Gottfried who shot him a stern glance.

He disappeared.

"He's right," Ben added sincerely. "When we offered our help, you said that you didn't have much choice and that it looked like you'd just have to make due."

"You are right," the King said seriously. "Firstly, this must be your choice—to help—selflessly, without thought of recognition or reward. It made no sense for me to puff you up. Secondly, you needed to discover your true power in steps and stages so that you would not be overwhelmed..."

Ben thought about what it would be like if they had been told everything from the beginning. 'Well,' he thought, 'then maybe we wouldn't have believed him. I'm not sure that we would have come.'

"This rescue has evolved to the point where more than just our gnomes must be saved. Much more is at stake now—more of our elemental friends are imprisoned with us, your parents are here, along with you, Dr. Abraham," he nodded in the scientist's direction.

"...And a major crystal that holds the vibratory balance for earth is now at risk of being exposed."

He looked at Ben, "Now is the time to use your power."

Chapter 52

High Tea

"More tea, Vincent?" Mary asked her quiet guest.

A teacup with cookies on a carefully folded handkerchief was laid out neatly before him. Her pink backpack was now placed beneath his still-swollen ankle. The stuffed animals that had previously been there were now sitting around a makeshift table she had made for the tea party.

Vincent didn't know quite what to do, so he politely sipped his tea and offered it for more as the opportunity arose.

For him, this was a far cry from his concentrated hours of research, but he kind of liked it.

The gemboard lit up again.

"Oh, I'll get it, Vincent!" Mary picked up the shell.

"Hello?" Queen Fiona called out.

"Hello, Queen Fiona," Mary hummed, "It's Mary. Can I help you?"

"Hello, Mary, dear," she answered. "King Hendrick has joined the three men, along with Ben and Jacob."

"We cannot see much," she explained, "but they seem to be safe at the moment. The king's rescue army has been fully captured."

"Vincent, are you there, too?" she asked.

"Ye-yes, your Highness," Vincent called out shyly.

"Good," the Queen continued, "Vincent, we have finally reached the Great Dragon Emperor of the Fire Kingdom. He knows our needs and will help as soon as he can, but he has much that he is dealing with as well."

"The fiery elementals are several miles below the surface, controlling the flow of magma beneath earth's tectonic plates. The diminishing of the mines is shifting the pressure on the layers of the earth. They are working so hard, the poor dears, to prevent serious earthquakes and volcanic eruptions…"

"I unders-s-stand," Vincent replied.

"Help is on its way, Vincent," the Queen encouraged.

"Please update Gottfried when he arrives. We will continue to monitor the situation from here and send you great thoughts of protection…" her voice trailed off.

"..and Vincent?" she said quietly.

"Yes, your Highness?" he replied.

"Remember the bats will help if called, as a last resort—if you have no choice but to give your location away."

"Yes, your Highness," Vincent answered confidently. "Not to fear. I will take good care of the daughter of man."

"Thank you," Queen Fiona replied.

"More tea?" Mary asked as she raised her water bottle up toward his cup.

"Ye-yes, please," Vincent graciously responded.

Chapter 53

Light Magic

"Gottfried," High King Hendrick called out quietly.

No response.

"Gottfried?" he called again.

Still nothing.

"Good," he sighed. He now turned to look toward his enslaved gnomes. Great sadness washed over him as he saw them slaving away on the various aspects of mine production.

He breathed in sharply several times as faces he had recognized came into view. He looked back to the table. He struggled to regain his composure.

Jacob looked out, then something caught his eye. He looked at the king. He looked out again.

"Your Highness," he uttered in astonishment, "look at the group of crystal sorters by the large rock. There must be fifty gnomes there. Do you see them?

The king and the others at the table looked over to see.

"No," the king replied truthfully, "they must have moved."

"With all due respect, your highness, they did not move. They were right there a moment ago."

They looked at each other.

"They disappeared!" Jacob tried to mask his excitement.

"He's right, Dad," Ben observed. Then he blinked and rubbed his eyes. "They're back!"

The gnomes had reappeared but this time there was something different. They began to stretch and yawn and look around them.

"It looks like they are waking up," Jacob whispered to the King.

"Very good," sighed the High King, "very good indeed."

"It's time we tried to help them," Ben said as he looked toward his father, uncle and Dr. Abraham.

They all closed their eyes with their heads on their hands, to look as if they were sleeping.

In the next moment, the gnomes disappeared again.

"King Hendrick," came Gottfried's hushed voice. "We need someone to lead the gnomes back to safety as we rescue them."

The King looked down and murmured his orders under his breath as if he were humming to himself. The guards looked over and then looked away to survey their newly captured creatures.

Had they noticed 50 missing gnomes?

Not yet.

Chapter 54

The Dark Alarm

In the next few moments, Jacob disappeared. Camp by camp, large groups of gnomes began to disappear.

Then, a whistle blew to announce the next workshift change.

Hundreds of gnomes began to emerge from tents to take the last set of gnome's workstations.

New guards emerged from the block buildings. They looked out to take note of the gnomes mining progress.

King Hendrick nodded toward the captives. The imprisoned animals saw his cue and began to kick up and make a scene. Birds flapped their wings and chirped and squawked. Animals raced back and forth, ramming themselves against the dark fence walls.

The guards, unaccustomed to any irregularity, raced past the mining areas to contain and calm their active new captives.

King Hendrick watched and planned as the last groups of gnomes disappeared. He quickly surveyed the scene to make sure all elderly, female and child-gnomes had left.

"It's time," he whispered softly so as not to break their concentration.

One of the guards noticed the king talking to the sleeping men and came nearer to silence him. Then, he suddenly looked around.

The disturbance made by the new prisoners had masked the fact that there was no longer any *tap-tap-tapping*. All workstations were abandoned. The gnomes were gone!

Red letter digital data began to flash across the guard's face and he pressed a lever on his side to sound an alarm.

Ee-ee-ee-ee-ee-ee-ee-ee…

"Gentlemen," the High King said, "stay focused and remain calm. Include us in the wall of light—now!"

In a second, they were gone.

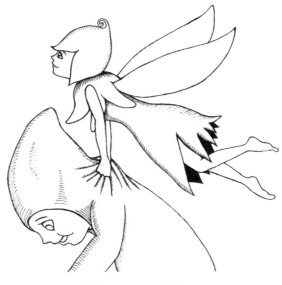

Chapter 55

Sweet Freedom

Inside the light, the men could see one another. They could see Ben beside them, heading toward the cave entrance. They could see George and Gottfried helping the last remaining gnomes up to the tunnel system with gnomes far ahead of them, moving at a very fast pace. They could also see King Hendrick, who had, instead, moved toward the captive army who had come to help set them free.

The men looked at Ben.

He nodded.

They knew what they had to do.

They included all of the birds, fairies and animals in the light.

The grey clouds began to brighten.

The fairies began to stretch and move. Soon, they were free from their bonds and quickly flew out the entrance. Fairies that were able picked up the young and elderly gnomes to help them back to safety quickly.

Next, the animals were freed.

The dark figures were flashing red. All were emitting loud alarm sounds. No matter how much grey energy they sent to any of the animals, it would dissipate quickly. They could not capture or hold them.

They could still see them, but there was nothing they could do.

Their power was gone.

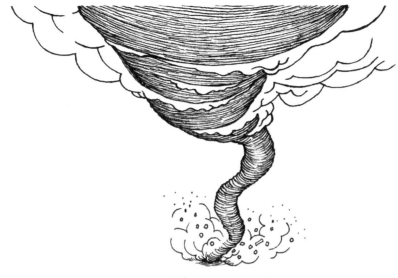

Chapter 56

Remember

All of a sudden the earth began to shake.

Black clouds and dust coalesced into a dark tornado in the center of the crystal cave.

The Wizards of Darkness had arrived in response to the alarms.

The walls continued to shake violently. All those still in the tunnel system held onto the walls, or each other, to keep their balance.

"Keep your faith!" High King Hendrick called out above the destructive tremors, "Press onward! We can do it!"

He urged them to stay calm and move on. They needed to evacuate the tunnels quickly.

George, Ben, their fathers and Dr. Abraham began to scoop up gnomes and carry them forward.

The air became thick with dark smoke. The tunnels continued to shake. A loud digital alarm echoed through the caverns. George and Ben looked at each other. They were afraid.

The smoked grew blacker with a sooty feel. They covered their mouths and pressed on.

"Wait," Ben remembered. "Remember the light!"

George began to remember the wall of light and began to see the caves full of fresh clean air.

Ben began to visualize everyone reaching safety and being completely free, with families reunited.

The air began to clear.

"Nice work, boys," Gottfried said as they passed him by. The alarms were muted—as if they were far, far away. The wall of light was protecting them.

"Where's Mary?" George's Dad asked as he came back from rescuing one of the last groups of gnomes.

"Oh!" the boys said in unison.

"She's back at the tent!"

Chapter 57

Safety First

"Eeeee, Eeeee!" the bats had arrived.

The tunnel walls were shaking and earth was falling down onto the tent. It was time to leave. Vincent knew what he had to do. Queen Fiona had alerted him to the most recent developments.

It was time to go.

Vincent swiftly packed the last of the equipment into Mary's pack. Both he and Mary would have to carry out what was absolutely necessary—the gem communication equipment, his instruments, maps, books and her stuffed animals.

Sigh.

The walls continued to shake.

He held Mary's hand tightly.

"I've been through things like this before Mary," said Vincent kindly. "Everything is going to be just fine."

"Okay..." Mary answered as bravely as she could.

It was all that that she could do to strain to hear the bats' echolocation sounds as they followed them through the falling tunnels.

Mary had tied a stuffed animal to their heads with ribbon, so any falling rock would not hurt at all.

Vincent reminded himself not to think about what he must look like. After all, it was a good idea.

Chapter 58

The Collapsing Tunnel

The last gnome was safely out in the open air.

Deer waiting to receive them whisked them away to a safe shelter. Due to the large numbers of rescued gnomes, many animals were needed to create a long convoy to escort them.

A long shaft of light surrounded them to hide them from the trees and unfriendly elements that were still under the spell of the Wizards' dark energy.

Like the stories of old, where the young boys traveled through the forest unnoticed by wolves and dark creatures, the gnomes escaped safely, without detection. The tunnels themselves were shifting and shaking and beginning to collapse.

Jacob nervously looked toward the mouth of the cave. His face brightened as Dr. Abraham stepped out, followed by High King Hendrick.

"Where are the others?" Jacob asked.

The High King took a labored breath before he could answer.

"Ben, George and their fathers ran back inside to find Mary and Vincent."

"Well, then, I must go, too!" volunteered Jacob, and before the King could protest, Jacob disappeared into the collapsing system of caves.

"Eeeee, Eeeee!" he heard as he moved forward through the shaking maze of rocks and falling debris.

"Eeeee, Eeeee!" the sound grew louder.

'The bats!' he said to himself.

"Vincent!" he shouted. "Are you there?"

"Ye-yes," he heard a faint response.

"We are here, too!" Jacob heard another voice coming from the other end of his tunnel.

"Is that you, Mr. Brent?" Jacob called back.

"Yes, we're here—keep shouting so that we can follow your

voice! We can't see anything anymore," George and Mary's dad explained. "We're looking for Mary."

"I'm here!" Mary called out.

"Thank goodness!" her father replied. "Honey, we'll be right there! Just hold on!"

Jacob took out his whistle from his pack and began to blow it frequently.

Both sets of voices grew nearer and nearer.

Finally, when they joined him it was completely dark. Not one flashlight was working. All the batteries had been used up. They needed to feel their way through, and with the help of the bats, they continued onward.

As Mary heard the voices grow nearer and nearer, she squealed with joy! She waved out her hands until she finally felt a shirt to hold onto.

"Who is this?" she called above the falling rubble.

"It's me, Mary," a kind voice replied. "It's Daddy."

Mary held him close and cried—tears that were not from fear or from sadness, but of gratitude and great love.

They continued on.

The cave seemed lighter somehow.

Chapter 59

The Great Battle

"Look, up ahead!" Vincent gasped.

"What is that?" his face instantly grew quite pale.

Red digits began to flash in the air. Black and grey smoke surrounded a large figure that began to become more and more concrete.

Jacob opened the penknife from his pack. He held it like a sword, preparing to defend all those behind him. He stepped forward.

A dark, mocking laugh pierced through the tunnel and resounded above the still-crumbling earth and falling rock.

"You have not won this day," it sneered.

The fathers stepped out before their children in defiance.

"Step aside and let us pass!" George and Mary's father shouted.

"We know what you are," Ben's father added, "You and all other Wizards of Darkness have no true power. Your days are numbered."

"Apparently, so are yours..." it replied arrogantly.

It, or he, laughed, "Let me give you an exact figure..." digital red numbers flew through the air, then a large number 10, then 9, then 8, then 7, then 6, then 5, then 4...grew large before them.

"Mary!" George called to her. "Pretend that there is white light around us, keeping us safe!"

"I can't," she replied, "I'm too scared!"

"Yes, you can," said Ben. "Just think about having a tea party inside a tent of white light!"

"Ye-yes, Mary," added Vincent, "I-I-I'd like that cup of tea now..."

"Oh!" cried Mary, "Okay!" and then she closed her eyes and pretended to see a tent of light around them.

The earth continued to shake. The men saw the numbers continue to 3, 2, and then 1. The men refused to give in to fear and joined the children in the visualization of light.

At "1," Jacob looked ahead.

The Wizard of Darkness was looking around the tunnel, confused, wondering where everyone had gone. But the entrance was now completely blocked by rocks and debris.

The Wizard's fury grew. He began to stab fiercely at the dark. When he realized that his efforts were in vain, he stopped. Confused and frustrated, he gathered up his darkness and vanished.

Then, suddenly, the tunnels stopped shaking. All was silent. They looked around them. There was no way out. The men looked at each other and did not say a word.

They were trapped, but they could not shake the feeling of being grateful to be alive.

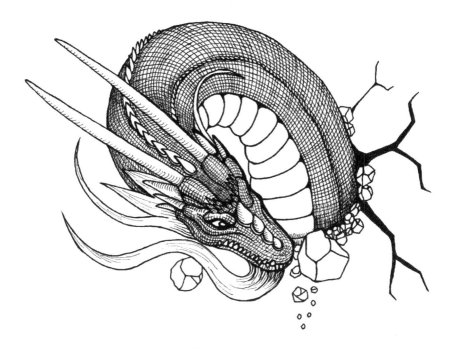

Chapter 60

A Surprising Way Out

Tap. Tap. Tap.

"Oh, no," George cried. "Did we miss someone? Is someone still trapped?"

Tap. Tap. Tap.

"I think someone is trying to communicate with us," Jacob said.

"Oh!" Vincent finally remembered. "I have the gemboard! Let me see if I can get someone!"

He knelt on the ground to try to search through his pack.

His ankle still hurt, but he ignored it for now. He found the pieces and hooked it up. "Hello?"

Maybe it was damaged from falling rock.

He spoke into it again, "Hello?"

"Hello!" called Queen Fiona. "Is that you, Vincent?"

"Ye-yes!" Vincent said proudly.

"I am so glad," she replied. "Let me locate you now on the map…" she said as they waited. "Your coordinates are up on the screen, Vincent. Who is there with you?"

"Jacob, Mary, Ben, George and their fathers," he listed.

"Wonderful. Is everyone alright?" she inquired.

"Yes," he replied happily.

"A rescue is on its way to you now," the Queen announced. "We shall see you very soon."

"Okay," Vincent replied, then shyly added, "Your Highness, I mean."

"Oh, please do not worry about formalities. Just get everyone back safely, my dear."

"I will," Vincent replied as a rumble began to sound through the cavern.

He quickly put the gemboard away and got ready.

The rumble grew louder and louder until they covered their ears from the intensity of the sound.

The earth started to shake and a large crack formed in the floor of the cavern. The fathers pulled everyone back toward the wall. Then up from the depths of the earth, a huge dragon appeared.

The great dragon was luminescent—with flashes of red, pink and orange. He had a long beard and fiery eyes. He did not speak, but continued upward, breaking a hole in the earth above him to create an exit that all could escape through.

They followed him up through the newly excavated tunnel and, one by one, they emerged to find High King Hendrick, Gottfried and Dr. Abraham anxiously awaiting their safe arrival. Dr. Abraham, however, did not take too much time to greet them. He could not take his eyes off the first dragon he had seen in his life.

Finally, everyone looked at Mary and Vincent.

"Nice hats," the boys said together.

Vincent looked up at the stuffed animal on his head. His face flushed with bright crimson.

Mary giggled and said, "Thank you!"

Chapter 61

Only the Beginning

The High King bowed low to the Great Dragon Emperor of the Fire Kingdom for rescuing his beloved friends. The rescue was complete, for now.

There were still many more mines to rescue gnomes from, and the Wizards of Darkness were not conquered, only temporarily thwarted.

Their day would come.

For now, the children were whisked back to the safety of the Great Tree. They were treated to tea and cake, warm lavender baths, fresh clothes and sleep.

The men and exhausted gnomes went up to the Great Room to discuss the day's events.

As they entered the room, the boys' fathers marveled at the advancements made in the technology there since their boyhood visits, while Dr. Abraham almost fainted with delight.

He walked slowly from wall to wall with sheer amazement and childlike delight. Finally, they sat down and learned of the depth and breadth of each elemental kingdom's current plight as outlined on each map.

Queen Fiona brought cups of hard acorn tea to sooth all nerves from all the excitement from the day. She complimented the men on the courage and integrity of their children, and then left them to continue in more serious discussion.

Man and gnome sat side-by-side, together in counsel with the hierarchies of each elemental kingdom to develop a united elemental strategy to end the suffering caused by the Chemical Kingdom.

It was time to create a change and restore balance.

King Hendrick was well pleased.

Man had entered the fight.

The End of Book One

The Elemental Kingdom
Book Series

Book Two: Water is next
in this adventure series.

Learn about the unseen forces
of nature and how change
is needed now to bring the
world back into balance.

Travel the globe with Ben,
Mary and George as they
learn ancient truths, meet
invisible friends and unravel
an incredible mystery along
the way.

Ready for the next quest?

Visit our web site for more information!
http://pamelahickein.wixsite.com/elementalkingdom

About the Author

Shhh... Don't tell anyone, but Pamela Sue Hickein is secretly a fairy, cleverly disguised as an artist, author, Master right brain teacher-trainer, mother and grandmother (her favorite jobs). Author of *Right Brain Education: How to Change the World: One Heart at a Time*, Hickein believes that the way to a child's mind is through creativity, imagination, play, lovingkindness and good humor. Pamela currently lives in North Carolina with her family, pets and fairy friends.

For more information about Pamela's work with right brain education, please visit rightbrainkids.com.

About the Illustrator

Siang Yang Ng is an amazing freelance artist from Kuala Lumpur, Malaysia. He is passionate about creating a better world through body (diet, nutrition), mind (creative education) and soul (art). He is currently a dietician, having completed a degree in Nutrition and Science.

In 2010, while teaching at a right-brain learning center in Asia, Siang Yang began to draw pictures to help excite children about learning to read. His illustrations are endearing to children—young and old.

Be kind.

FROG & TURTLE
CHILDREN'S PRESS

Made in the USA
Middletown, DE
26 November 2022

16094364R00109